"Laura, Laura, ... first we were meant to be lovers," Devlin said in a husky whisper

Devlin's startling assertion slapped Laura back to reality. What did she think she was doing? "Devlin!" she cried out. "Don't say that! I—I didn't come to Ireland to have an affair with a stranger!"

"Neither did I, Laura," he assured her, his soft-spoken affirmation granting her a ray of hope that he, too, had regained his senses.

But when he looked at her, his eyes were filled with desire. Indeed, his expression held no acknowledgment of her rejection, no hint that he didn't fully intend for them to writhe naked together, very soon, tangled blissfully in clean Irish sheets tucked away in some quaint inn. He flashed her a roguish grin that provoked wayward and wanton impulses in her.

Laura swallowed hard, experiencing both dread and anticipation. She stared into his handsome, confident face, unable to speak or move. The bold glitter in his eyes was promising that Laura *would* have an affair with a stranger in Ireland—and that stranger would be Devlin Rafferty.

Renee Roszel became a professional writer at the tender age of ten; her hometown newspaper paid her five dollars for a feature titled "My Pop Is Tops." However, her career didn't really take off until her two sons started school. She decided to try writing romance novels and hasn't looked back since. Renee lives in Tulsa, Oklahoma, with her husband.

Acknowledgment

I want to thank a fellow writer, and "lover of all things Irish," Suzanne Barrett, for her assistance in helping me make this story as authentically Irish as possible. Suzanne has traveled extensively in Ireland and has publishing credits over there that include everything from an article on farmhouse cheeses to romantic fiction. She laughingly calls herself "the fake Irishman," but more seriously says the first time she set foot on the Emerald Isle, she felt as though she'd come home. She hopes to retire there one day. My wish for her is that she will.

Thanks, also, to William O'Donnell, a fine Irish-American gentleman who generously assisted when called upon, and who made me laugh, his charm and whimsy as enchanting as the leprechauns of his land.

To both Suzanne and William, I say with all my heart—*Cead mile failte!*

SEX, LIES
AND LEPRECHAUNS
RENEE ROSZEL

Harlequin Books

TORONTO • NEW YORK • LONDON
AMSTERDAM • PARIS • SYDNEY • HAMBURG
STOCKHOLM • ATHENS • TOKYO • MILAN
MADRID • WARSAW • BUDAPEST • AUCKLAND

If you purchased this book without a cover you should be aware that this book is stolen property. It was reported as "unsold and destroyed" to the publisher, and neither the author nor the publisher has received any payment for this "stripped book."

To
Jerod and Shannon Lyles
and
Natalie, Nikki and Scott Roszel
Love,
Aunt Renée

ISBN 0-373-25583-7

SEX, LIES AND LEPRECHAUNS

Copyright © 1994 by Renee Roszel Wilson.

All rights reserved. Except for use in any review, the reproduction or utilization of this work in whole or in part in any form by any electronic, mechanical or other means, now known or hereafter invented, including xerography, photocopying and recording, or in any information storage or retrieval system, is forbidden without the written permission of the publisher, Harlequin Enterprises Limited, 225 Duncan Mill Road, Don Mills, Ontario, Canada M3B 3K9.

All characters in this book have no existence outside the imagination of the author and have no relation whatsoever to anyone bearing the same name or names. They are not even distantly inspired by any individual known or unknown to the author, and all incidents are pure invention.

This edition published by arrangement with Harlequin Enterprises B. V.

® and TM are trademarks of the publisher. Trademarks indicated with ® are registered in the United States Patent and Trademark Office, the Canadian Trade Marks Office and in other countries.

Printed in U.S.A.

1

DEVLIN RAFFERTY WAS very near smiling—something he hadn't felt much like doing ever since he'd slammed out of his office two weeks ago, brimming with anger and guilt. But here, in this improbable place—Customs in Ireland's Shannon Airport—he felt a spark of genuine amusement. Unfortunately, it was at the expense of the young woman in front of him.

He watched as she tried to explain to a customs agent how her TV remote-control device had ended up in her suitcase.

She was an unlikely-looking terrorist, he decided, scanning her from the top of her wildly curly, taffy-colored hair, to her comfortable flat shoes. The madras sundress she wore wasn't nearly adequate enough for the damp chill of Ireland in early May. Clearly, she was from somewhere in the States that was quite warm already, and had no idea how inappropriately she was dressed.

The woman, who looked to be in her early thirties, was slender and petite—probably no more than five-three. Her short, fitted sundress allowed a generous glimpse of shapely athletic legs, and though he hadn't been in the mood to give much of a damn about any woman's legs lately, he found himself considering this particular set of feminine limbs with growing interest. Her troubled tone of voice, however, brought him back to her dilemma.

"Look . . ." She ran both hands through her hair, plainly fit to be tied by the customs agent's suspicious attitude. "I swear to you, I don't know how my remote got in my suitcase. Maybe because I packed in a rush. For Pete's sake," she lamented, "I'm not dangerous!"

The pug-nosed customs agent inspected her with trained distrust. "Ah, and I'm supposed to be takin' yer word on that, missy?" he demanded sardonically. "Just last month I caught me a rosy-cheeked granny with a pound of plastique in her grip. She swore to me face, says she, the stuff was modeling clay fer her grandbaby. 'Isn't that fine,' says I. Then I packed her off to jail, that I did. So don't try to play the innocent with me." He placed the remote aside and set about investigating her belongings with bulldog determination, as though he'd single-handedly unearthed the ringleader of a revolutionary plot.

As the agent carelessly excavated through her suitcase, the young woman, her cheeks flaming with indignation, attempted to grab at a dangling bra, but the resolute agent halted her with, "If ye don't mind, you're ta keep yer hands clear whilst I do me duty."

She glanced furtively about, catching Devlin's perusal. "What do you think you're staring at?" she flared.

He couldn't resist a crooked grin at her nerve. "Sorry." Without further comment, he turned away, but only slightly. He could still see her out of the corner of his eye.

"Ah, and what's this?" the agent asked with evil glee as he held up a plastic bag filled with a white powdery substance.

"It—it's soap flakes," she said. "Is there a law against soap flakes?"

"'Tis only yer word. Could be drugs."

Devlin heard a gasp and shifted to face the woman again.

"Drugs?" she echoed, her voice incredulous. "I'll have you know that's Madam Lupeck's Hypoallergenic Soap Chips for—" She paused, then leaned closer to the agent, but not near enough to prevent Devlin from hearing. "It's for my delicate underthings," she whispered urgently. "I'm allergic to detergents, and the giant, economy-size box was too big to pack. You see...I, er, get a rash...."

The agent nodded. "I see. Yer sayin' 'tis only soap." He nodded again. "Then it won't harm yer things, I'll be thinkin'."

As he spoke, he opened the bag and dumped the white flakes all over the disordered contents of her gaping suitcase.

A customs agent standing nearby gave a reproachful cough and nudged his companion as though in disapproval. Devlin could understand why. This was decidedly shabby conduct for an Irishman. But, customs men the world over were a breed apart. He supposed they had to be tough and suspicious in their jobs. That very suspiciousness probably saved thousands of lives in the long run. But in this case, Devlin doubted the agent had needed to be quite so contrary.

As soap coated her belongings, the young woman shrieked with dismay and did a little dance of disaster that would have been charming and whimsical under other circumstances, Devlin thought. Even in her anguish, she bore the quaintest resemblance to one of Ireland's own little people, jigging there on her pixie feet, her hands fluttering about her animated face. But if she did slightly resemble a leprechaun, she was far from being a happy one.

The miserable young woman was obviously a first-time overseas tourist, not knowing any better than to transport such questionable items as unmarked white powder and remote-control devices in a suitcase. He wondered what else she might be hauling, and hoped, for her own sake, she had no lighters shaped like handguns among her lacy, hypoallergenic undies. Otherwise she might find herself spending her vacation in an Irish jail.

"How *dare* you!" she cried, aghast. "You've got soap all over my clothes. And how am I supposed to wash out my—my—"

"I'll have to confiscate your detonating device, miss," the agent interrupted brusquely.

"It's not a detonating—"

"Don't back-answer me, young lady. Move along with ya, now," he barked.

She stood, disbelieving. "What?"

Devlin had never seen a face so confused and upset, yet somehow endearing. She simply couldn't accept what had just happened. He decided he'd better step in before she got herself into more trouble. Moving forward and arranging her things in the bag so it could be closed, he shut it, addressing her quietly, "The man said you may go." Placing the case in her hand, he added in a whisper, "I'd get out of here before he changes his mind."

"But—but he's got my TV remote," she protested, the heftiness of the bag apparently bringing her out of her stupor.

"Yes, he has your remote," Devlin said with grim earnestness. "And he could have your butt, if he wanted. Consider yourself lucky. In this day and age, airport customs agents take battery-operated devices and druglike substances *damned* seriously. Apparently he's decided you're not so much dangerous as you are foolish."

Her gold-brown eyes widened. "Who do you think you are, calling me fool—"

"Move along, missy," the agent chided. "I've got me work ta do."

She looked back at the customs man. "Do you mean to tell me you're really not going to give me back my—"

"Look, lady," Devlin said, purposefully harsh. It was clear to everyone but her that she was on the verge of exchanging her unfortunate introduction into international travel for a little lockup time. He interjected with the only excuse he could think of: "You may have all day, but I don't." Jerking his head toward the exit, he said, "Move along, like the man said."

She clamped her mouth shut and glared at him. When she made no move to go, he asided in a warning growl, "If you have the brains of a fungus, you'll get the hell out of here."

A dismaying shimmer formed in her lower lashes. "I don't know about my brain—sir—" she began in a firm, though emotion-tinged voice "—but you definitely have the *charm* of a fungus!" Her expression stark and proud, she spun around and tramped off.

Devlin, who'd been wallowing in his own misery for the past several weeks, had suddenly had a glimpse of someone else's pain—and he felt like a louse for how he'd treated her. His only excuse was, he hadn't had time to work out a more kindly scenario. Well. At least she was out of trouble and on her not-so-merry way.

With odd reluctance, Devlin returned his attention to the customs agent. As he waited to be allowed through, he found it impossible to think about anything else but a certain impish, spitfire of a woman who hated his guts.

LAURA TODD HADN'T HAD the best day of her life by any stretch of the imagination. She stood on the ancient cobblestones of the coach yard of the Dingle Bay Country House Hotel, gazing up at the ashen facade of a squat sixteenth-century gatehouse tower, choked with ivy. She could hardly concentrate on the sight before her—she was still enraged by her encounter with that utterly rude, dark-haired man in the bomber jacket and jeans at the airport. How dare he suggest she had the brains of a fungus. What a jerk! She attempted to calm herself by reminding herself that her room was in a lovely gatehouse with the sweetest turret, and completely secluded from the main hotel. Just knowing she'd be staying here took the edge off her annoyance.

One had to be nimble and young to be consigned the gatehouse room, she'd discovered, after the portly proprietor had stepped inside the door and merely pointed up to it, assisting as well as he could while she struggled up with her bags. He'd said they'd ordered timber and were going to put in a real staircase, soon. But right now, gaining entrance required its occupant to climb a ladder to reach the bedroom loft. But what a joyous sight the climb up the rickety steps brought: a centuries-old stone fireplace and Spartan, white-painted furnishings. The brass bed was covered by a lively patchwork quilt, and hand-painted crockery vases, overflowing with wildflowers, were set out on the mismatched chests and dressing table. A sheepskin rug lay invitingly before the hearthstone.

Laura had her own bath, thankfully, and though there was a telephone and electricity for lighting, there was no TV or radio—which suited her just fine.

The first thing she'd done in that wonderful room was to change into jeans and a sweater. Dingle Bay was cool, bordering on cold to a Florida native, but the whole place was so breathtaking she would have stood on the grounds stark naked in a snowstorm if she'd had to, just to have the opportunity to see it.

The country house's owner, Quillan Phelan, had met her and an elderly couple at the airport with his ancient hotel bus. She'd been terrified during the ride from Shannon, unable to sit calmly in a bus chugging down the "wrong" side of the winding roads.

But even during the harrowing ride to the hotel, she'd been entranced by the Dingle Bay landscape. The high cliffs overlooking the bay were sprinkled with purple heather and saffron-yellow gorse—or so Quillan had called the prickly shrub, which gave off a brilliant hue as it danced in the sea breezes.

The country house itself, built in the late 1800s, had been constructed on the original foundations and walls of a four-hundred-year-old castle. The imposing facade of the three-story hotel was softened by a lavish veil of purple wisteria that also cloaked much of the old castle's tumbledown ramparts. A sweet-scented profusion of roses, rhododendrons, tulips, pansies and greenery was crisscrossed by walkways formed of stones from the castle ruins. This "palace patch" as Quillan had so quaintly called it, was an enchanting sweep of flowers and scents.

Laura sighed with appreciation, overwhelmed by the whole old-world experience. Ireland was turning out to be a more picturesque and delightful place than she'd

imagined—except for their customs department...
and one irritating American tourist!

Unable to ignore the misty-cold sea breeze one second longer, Laura headed back into the gatehouse, and was halfway up the rickety ladder to her room when her damp loafer slid out from under her and her leg plunged through the slat, causing her to lose her balance and pitch backward. Her bent leg caught her and she dangled there, her hair grazing the stone floor. As she squealed in fright, a shadow appeared in the gatehouse doorway.

It was the silhouette of a man. Even upside down and in the semidarkness, she could tell he was a magnificent specimen, with a wide set of shoulders and, from her close proximity to his jeans-clad thighs, she determined that his lower extremities were far from scrawny, too.

"Are you all right?" he asked, his deep voice tense.

With blood rushing to her head, and feeling like an idiot, she blurted defensively, "*Sure.* I'm fine. I'm just waiting for a bus!"

She heard him clear his throat as though masking amusement. "Forgive me," he murmured. "That 'Are you all right' crack was uncalled-for."

Though he'd sounded amused, she couldn't miss the censure in his tone. Just as she was about to suggest that what she needed right now was help, not a lecture, she felt herself being lifted until she was upright enough to extract her trapped leg. Then, strong arms helped her to stand. When she could focus on his face, she sputtered in breathless disbelief, "Not—*you!*"

He lounged there against the wall, wearing the same bomber jacket and the same worn jeans: *the dark-*

haired jerk from the airport. With an inquiring tilt of his head, he said, "I gather you remember me."

"It's coming back to me," she said grimly. "Weren't you on last week's episode of 'America's Most Wanted'?"

He grinned. "Apparently your day hasn't gotten much better since Customs."

"It was going *fine* until this minute. How did you get *here,* anyway?"

"Rented a car." He shrugged, shoving his hands into his hip pockets. "By the way, you're welcome."

She felt a rush of annoyance at his sarcasm. But he was right. He had come along at a time when she'd needed help—this time, anyway. She might have ended up with a concussion without him. Reining in her anger, she muttered, "I suppose I owe you my thanks."

He extended a hand. "You're welcome, again. I'm Devlin Rafferty. Chicago."

She took it, but only briefly. "Laura Todd, Tallahassee, Florida."

"Vacation?" he asked.

She shook her head. "Business."

He seemed a bit surprised. "Oh? What do you do?"

A cool sea breeze wafted in, causing Laura to shiver. "I... Look, Mr. Rafferty. I was just about to change for dinner and—"

"You're cold. Did Quillan stoke your peat fire?"

She was at a loss and evidently showed it. "I'll do it for you." Before she could protest, he was up the ladder and inside her room.

She clambered after him. "Now, look, Mr. Rafferty, I don't just allow any man to come into my room, you know."

He stoked the peat, adding a couple of bricks of fuel. "What kind of business brings you to Ireland?" he asked, ignoring her reproach and pulling up one of two white-painted chairs. Straddling its seat, he crossed his arms over the scarred back, "I think drugs and terrorism have been pretty much ruled out," he remarked wryly.

She'd been just about to excuse his earlier rudeness, but his reminder of her humiliation at Customs revived her hostility. Jutting her chin, she stated, "Don't let me keep you if you have to be going."

She came over beside him, not because she wanted to be near this disturbing man, but because she'd been cold enough today, and the heat of the fire was very appealing.

"What's this?" he asked, plucking something from the shoulder of her sweater.

"What's what?" She peered at him with distrust.

"Oh." A dark brow arched in mischief. "I think I've captured one of your illegal soap flakes."

She flushed, snatching at it. "I spent—I don't know how long—sifting that stuff from my clothes and saving all I could. You'd think it was less funny if you . . . if you . . ." She let the words die away, having no intention of discussing her sensitive skin with this man. Her personal life was *personal*.

"You get a rash, I know," he said. "I overheard you tell the customs agent. I hope you could save most of your soap."

Odd. He sounded serious, as though he were genuinely concerned. "I'll let you get dressed for dinner," he offered without a trace of teasing, moving toward the ladder.

Startled by his sudden metamorphosis, she didn't know how to react. She was about to say something completely civil, when he asked, "Laura, do you believe in love at first sight?"

She stared. "Do I believe in—what?"

He was halfway down the ladder. Then, watching her closely with blue eyes that were strangely sad, he leaned forward, his elbows on the uneven oak-plank floor. "Love at first sight. Do you believe in it?"

Her words set off a confusion of emotions. Laura wasn't sure whether she was exhilarated or panicked. "I'd believe in leprechauns before I'd believe in such nonsense," she responded thinly, surprised by her own violent response to a question that was most likely harmless.

He continued to observe her for a moment, but Laura could read nothing of his thoughts. After a minute, he cautioned, "I wouldn't anger the little people if I were you. They do exist—as surely as does love at first sight."

Before she could form a pithy rejoinder, he was gone. The door squeaked closed as he exited the gatehouse, leaving behind no sound but the sizzle of the peat fire. Suddenly she didn't feel all that pithy. Surely he hadn't meant... But there had been *something* in his tone that suggested . . .

No. It was silly! He didn't mean her—that he'd fallen in love with *her* at first sight! To steady herself, Laura grabbed the back of the chair he'd been occupying, and perched on the cane seat.

She had to give him credit. The man had a charming line—almost as charming as the compelling sensuality of his blue stare. On the other hand, he was mouthy and pushy; and he radiated an air of unhappiness.

Slumping against the hard slats of the chair back, she closed her eyes and inhaled. Even considering all his obvious faults, she had a feeling it would take a little doing to forget Mr. Rafferty's sexy, somber eyes. But she would forget them. She'd put him and this whole bizarre episode out of her mind. She was here on business, and she had an important job to do.

PERPLEXED, LAURA STOOD before the sumptuous groaning board filled with delicious-smelling dishes. She hesitated, wondering what several of the choices were. She recognized the vegetables, the baked turkey, roast pork and beef, the various breads and cheeses, but there were several other things . . .

"That's sea urchin in mayonnaise," came a familiar deep voice.

She turned around to see the annoying Devlin Rafferty, dressed now in a neat pair of charcoal wool slacks and a dove-gray crewneck sweater. He looked pressed and neat and awfully tall, standing there towering over her. She noticed he had no plate.

"Aren't you eating?" she asked.

"I've served myself. And since we're both here alone, I thought we might eat together." He nodded toward a nearby doorway. "I'm at a table in that anteroom." He half grinned in invitation.

She swallowed. "Well, er—"

"I'd recommend the stuffed mussels, if you've never tried them. They're a specialty here."

"How do you know so much about the food here?"

"I visited with my folks several times when I was growing up. Things don't change much from decade to decade." His expression sobered. "I suppose that's why I came back."

She considered his words. The man was definitely harboring some sort of heartache. Probably just divorced or widowed. How sad for him. Compassion tempering her original opinion, she decided he probably had some inner pain that he was trying to heal. Taking pity, she said, "Okay, the stuffed mussels and the anteroom to the left?"

A spark of what seemed like surprise flashed in his eyes. "May I help carry something?"

She noticed a plate of scones, a particular weakness of hers. "Could you get me one of those?"

When he had, she went with him into the small chamber to the side of the main dining room. It was a pleasant, intimate spot with a low, beamed ceiling and dark oak-paneled walls. There were only three tables in the room, two of them each occupied by two elderly couples. Heavy wine-and-green damask drapes had been drawn across the large, arched window, and bookshelves filled with ancient-looking leather-bound volumes covered the opposite wall. Swathing the dark wood floor was a fine old needlepoint rug in a dusky floral design.

The only vacant table was situated by the carved marble fireplace. Laura felt a surge of gratitude for Devlin's consideration. She'd thought that her cotton sweater-dress would be plenty warm, even though it didn't quite reach her knees. But despite the cotton tights she'd put on, she could feel the chill of the Irish evening. Laura's attitude toward Devlin Rafferty was warming as rapidly as her skin.

She sat down feeling unsure of where things were leading. He unnerved her with that sexy, doleful gaze and his all-too-gentlemanly act. She almost wished he'd call her "fungus brain" again. It would be safer. She thought again of his earlier question about love at first sight, then put the idea from her mind. There was nothing to be gained by dwelling on such a crazy subject.

She had no intention of becoming involved with a man—any man—until he proved himself in one very important way. A secret test. And neither had she any intention of spilling her guts about her personal life. She hated to see disgust or pity in a man's face. Her new rule was to keep her mouth shut and her private life off-limits. So, she'd have dinner with Devlin, and she'd have polite conversation with Devlin, but she wouldn't give off 'I'm available' vibrations, and would steel herself against the all-too-arousing vibes he was putting out. She glanced up at him as his chair scraped along the edge of the rug, indicating he was taking his seat.

Their gazes met and he gave her that half smile again.

"What is it that you do that brings you to Ireland?" he asked without preamble.

"What are you, a lawyer? You come on with such direct questions—like you're cross-examining me," she said, smiling with exasperation.

"You're very sharp. I was a lawyer," he admitted, frowning. "Right now I'm unemployed."

She felt a tremor of worry. Had he been disbarred? Was he a criminal? Had he skipped out of the States with the police hot on his heels? She was quiet, not knowing what to say.

"Sorry. Guess I need to learn to just talk to people again." She gave him a brief look as he sipped his coffee. When he'd replaced his cup in the saucer, he said, "You choose the subject."

To stall, she took a forkful of her minted peas. When she swallowed, she asked, only half kidding, "Er—are you on the run from the Feds or what?"

He choked on a bite of his stuffed mussels, "When you pick a subject, you pick a subject."

She took another forkful of peas, waiting.

He inspected her ruefully. "No. I'm not wanted. I quit. Came to Dingle Bay to think—sort out what I want to do with my life."

She didn't know if she should, but she believed him. Sipping her coffee, she scanned the fire. After a minute she said, "I haven't been here long, but it does seem like it would be a good place to think. It's so serene and—and somehow untouched."

He smiled, then. It was a melancholy piece of work, but it was dashing in its way. Laura felt its effect. "Yes, *untouched* is a good word." He nodded. "And pure..."

She watched him in silence for a long time as he ate. She wasn't sure if he knew he was being observed or not. He seemed to have traveled somewhere else for a time—somewhere very grim. Finally, deciding there was no real reason for her not to tell him why she was in Ireland, at least—she owed him that much for the warm fire and for the rescue—she cleared her throat. "I work for the Abandoned Property Division of the Florida Treasury Department."

His inspection grew curious, but he didn't speak, so she went on, "I'm what they call an heir hunter. My boss has always taken the overseas jobs, but he's recuperating from a triple bypass, so I got this one."

Devlin studied her. "An heir hunter?" he repeated. "I don't think I've ever heard of that before."

She relaxed a little. Her job was one of the aspects of her life she didn't mind talking about. "Most of the time my duties consist of tracking down people who have forgotten about old bank accounts or stocks, or lost beneficiaries of paid-up insurance policies. It's mainly chasing leads by digging through birth and death records. Employment and police records."

She paused to take a breath and crossed her legs. Her foot brushed against his calf, and she shifted, embarrassed by the unexpected contact. Hoping he couldn't detect the flush that suddenly warmed her cheeks, she hurried on, "You know—the paper trails most of us leave. Fairly unglamorous, tedious paper shuffling, phone calls and legwork. Still, it's a rewarding career. Did you know, for instance, that one person out of about ten in this country has unclaimed cash waiting in state treasuries? Most of it's small stuff—anywhere from a dollar or two to a hundred. But then there are those few cases that amount to a fortune. In my office alone, there's more than $200 million in money that rightfully belongs to heirs who can't be located, and more millions come rolling in all the time."

Devlin raised a brow. "Interesting."

She couldn't tell if he really thought it was interesting or not. But should it matter? She loved her work, and that's all that was important. Laura found it satisfying to help people recover lost or owed funds, so what did she care what a temporary dinner companion might think? She went on, "My boss's motto is, 'There's somebody out there for everybody.'"

Devlin smiled mildly. "He sounds like a romantic."

She shook her head at the idea of her cynical, ex-cop boss as anything remotely akin to a romantic. At least not judging by his crusty, growling attitude around the office. But she supposed anyone who chased down heirs for a living must have a certain romance deep in his

soul. "Maybe," she conceded. "But the remark refers
to the fact that no matter how cold the trail might be,
there's somebody out there connected to every person.
A good investigator doesn't quit until he, or she, finds
that connection."

"So you're over here looking for some human connection to a long-lost heir?"

She nodded. "It's an intriguing mystery. And with my
boss's surgery only two weeks ago, he was in no con-
dition to travel, so it came at the right time for me to
have a great opportunity to right an old wrong." She
paused, then smiled wistfully. "I've never been as-
signed such a big case—and I've never traveled out of
the United States before—well, except for a week on my
honey—" She halted, then veered back to the subject
at hand. "Anyway, I'm lucky to have been given this
case, and grateful that my boss thinks I can handle it."
She *would* succeed, too! If she did, it could mean a
promotion, and the money would come in handy now
that Sally was almost school-age. She'd need—

"I gather the trail's cold," he said, breaking into her
thoughts.

"Frozen." She sighed, welcoming the interruption.
"And to make matters worse, I don't have much to go
on. Not even the sex. All I know is the child's mother's
name is Kathleen and that she worked as a housemaid
here at Dingle Bay Country House Hotel some thirty-
six years ago. The child is Irish and the father is—was—
an American film director."

"No kidding," Devlin said, his sad blue eyes reflect-
ing genuine interest. "Who was the director?"

"His name was Josh Kincade. Ever hear of him?"

Devlin sat back, his expression contemplative. "Didn't he direct that Vietnam movie that got an Oscar back in the seventies?"

"He got several in his career, I understand. He even got a nomination for the movie he directed over here when he made the mysterious Kathleen pregnant—the bastard."

Devlin frowned. "Name-calling, are we?"

"Well, in his will he admitted she asked him for his help and that he refused her. Didn't want his wife to know. But after all these years he felt guilty. His wife was dead and all, and they never had any children." She shrugged. "He admitted he'd been a bastard."

"Point taken. By the way, are you married? That ring on your left hand doesn't look quite like a wedding ring."

Another one of those personal questions out of the blue. Instinctively her guard flew up. She had an urge to tell him it was none of his business, but decided that particular fact didn't matter that much. "Divorced. The ring was my grandmother's." *And that's all you get*, she vowed.

"That explanation had a period on it if I ever heard one. Don't want to talk about it?"

She retrieved her fork and poked at her stuffed mussels without comment.

"None of my business?" he queried.

She took a bite, chewed, then asked, "Is it going to be this cold all the time here in Ireland?"

He assumed one of his cynical smiles. "Okay, Ms. Todd, whatever you say." Lounging back, he said with studied nonchalance, "Here's a thought. Why don't we talk about the weather? In case you're interested, Ireland can be very nice in May, but it can also be cool and wet."

"Are *you*?" she interrupted suddenly.

"Am I what? Wet?" he replied with faint amusement.

Her cheeks grew hot. Her mind had careened down a wayward path, and, unfortunately her mouth had followed. "I—uh—no." She stammered, unable to think of a smooth segue. "I was wondering if you're married—or divorced, or anything?"

An unaccountable look of withdrawal, even hatred, came over his features. "I've never been married—except, maybe, to my work." His tone harsh, he added, "Now, I'm divorced from that."

"I've stumbled into one of those 'none of your business' areas, haven't I?" Laura asked, feeling as though she'd probed at the very core of his sadness and slashed open a wound. "I'm sorry."

He chuckled, the sound bitter. "Hell. Don't worry about it. It's just that—the thing's a little fresh. . . ." He glanced away, and Laura could tell he was attempting to maintain his composure. After a few seconds he grinned at her, a contemptuous fraud of a grin. "So much for Old Home Week," he quipped tersely, as he rose to his feet. "How about a piece of raspberry-jam cake?"

"Okay, thanks."

She knew he needed a minute alone, and the pretense of retrieving dessert was as good an excuse as any to get away. She watched his retreat from the corner of her eye. He was outwardly self-possessed and as handsome as the devil. Watching him stroll by, no one would guess how broken-up he was inside.

What had happened to Devlin Rafferty? What had been so tragic that he'd abandoned his life's work and traveled across an ocean to try to forget?

2

As THEY ATE THEIR desserts, Laura felt the strain between them. It was plain that Devlin's hurt was hovering barely beneath the surface and was intensely painful. She cast about for some safe topic—one that wouldn't take them in the direction of either her personal sorrows or his.

Her attention was drawn to two large portraits that hung above the fireplace. They were not of a husband and wife, as she would have expected. One was of a foppish, redheaded hunchback dressed in the brocade and silk-stockinged style of two hundred years past. Beside this grotesque gentleman hung the portrait of a jester, wearing a striped pointed hat, garish costume and elfin shoes. Wondering aloud rather than attempting conversation, Laura remarked, "What a bizarre coupling."

"My, my," Devlin said, his tone peculiar. When she shifted to face him, he wore a curious smile. Though his eyes reflected no contentment, they beckoned in their somber way. "Are we having kinky fantasies?"

She frowned, confused, then recalled what she'd said and how her mumbled thought must have sounded, coming out of the blue like that. Even so, she didn't plan to let him get away with such an insinuation. From unpleasant past experiences, she knew that was one way men tested a woman's sexual availability—an erotic innuendo here, a sly, seemingly casual remark there.

Then, *wham-o!* The oh-baby-I-think-we-could-be-fab-together lunge. The only reason she wasn't eating in her room—precisely to avoid this type of thing—was because the Dingle Bay Country House didn't offer such a service.

In her eight years with the Florida Treasury Department, she'd traveled enough in her job to be aware that lots of men, lonely and away from home, went as far as they could sexually. A guy might test a woman's reaction to a mildly lewd remark, and if she remained casual and smiling, he'd test her further. Then the first thing you knew, he'd be pawing her and insisting she knew she wanted it and was a heartless tease if she objected!

Well, Laura *did* object, and Devlin Rafferty might as well know it now as later. She clanked her fork to her plate of half-eaten pastry, and informed him, "Let's get one thing straight, Mr. Rafferty. I travel a lot in my business, and I've been hit on by plenty of jerks. I don't play little out-of-town sex games in hotels. The only reason I'm here with you is because—because I thought I owed you something for saving my brains earlier today. But don't kid yourself that you'll get more from me than polite conversation. My kinky fantasies—if and when I have them—are none of your business. Is that understood? We're having dinner and that's *all* we're having."

During her tirade, his eyes narrowed. When she'd finished, he said almost harshly, "Is that everything you wanted to tell me?"

"I just hope I've made myself clear," she added, feeling a little embarrassed for such a heated outburst. She hadn't meant to snap at the man. He obviously had plenty of unhappiness in his life. Still, that didn't exempt him from jerkdom, she supposed. Somewhere, deep inside, she felt a tug of disappointment about that.

She hated to admit it, but something basic in her was struggling with an attraction for Devlin that had begun the instant she'd seen him in that dratted customs line—an attraction that was powerful and full-bodied. And her real reason for eating with him had a bit more to do with that stupid attraction than any small degree of gratitude. Too bad he was an everyday run-of-the-mill creep. Oh, well. She found herself sighing aloud. "Have I?" she asked. "Made myself clear, that is?"

"Let me see." He sat back, outwardly relaxed. "You're saying we aren't going to run naked in the fields and have wild, mindless sex on the croquet lawn after dinner, as I'd planned?"

His tone and his description of such a ridiculous escapade made her feel silly for having come on so strong. "I gather you're saying I—overreacted a little."

He shrugged, sitting forward. "Listen, Laura. Since you've been straight with me, I'll be straight with you, okay? I'd be happy to have hot sex with you—maybe not on the croquet lawn. It's too chilly right now. But, if the topic comes up again, and you're not interested, a simple 'No' will work. Am *I* clear?"

He waited for her to respond, the firelight accentuating his square jaw and handsome features. His eyes held hers and she sensed the truth in his words. She was startled that he'd admitted that having sex with her interested him. Once so soundly rejected, most men looking for a one-night fling would have attempted to soothe their tattered egos by sneering that she had a pretty overblown idea of her allure and stalked off. *Jerks.* But Devlin hadn't done that, and as a result she found herself trusting him a little more, liking him even better. If he'd denied being attracted, she'd never have been able to believe a word that came out of his mouth. But his interest had been evident in his eyes, in his invitation to dinner and—and that remark in the loft. . . .

She thought again of his words, *"Do you believe in love at first sight?"* She had to admit that she had, once. It had happened to her in her life. But she'd found out the hard way that it didn't mean "happily ever after."

Not by a long shot.

She heard a voice and was pulled from her reverie. "What?" she asked.

He was watching her with those erotic blue eyes. "You didn't answer me. Did *I* make myself clear?"

She nodded her head in agreement. "Oh—yes—and, I appreciate your frankness."

"I'd like to think we could always be honest with each other, Laura."

She nodded again, deciding they could—as long as he kept his questions directed away from her personal life. She had no intention of talking about Vincent or Matt—or, especially, little Sally.

"Do you think you could tell me now—" he cleared his throat, easing into what had been a sore subject only minutes ago "—what you meant by 'bizarre coupling'?"

She found herself flushing. All this fuss over a mumbled comment about the placement of a pair of paintings. "It's not that interesting. I was wondering why those two guys are hanging over the fireplace together. Not exactly the typical Irish couple, I hope."

He surveyed the canvases, then laughed. "Ah, that's old Master Ahern, the eighteenth-century squire of this place, and one of his jesters." Devlin turned back to look at her. "Every great house had a jester back then to help while away dull nights."

A perverse voice inside her insisted, *I doubt if nights whiled away with you would ever be dull, Devlin Rafferty.* Suddenly she was overcome with the urge to giggle. *Enough mental silliness!* she groused, struggling to stand. "Oh—well, that's interesting. I'd better be getting on to sex—" She bit her lip, praying he hadn't heard her Freudian slip. "To *sleep*," she corrected herself firmly. "I need to check the bus schedule and be in Dingle first thing tomorrow. One of the Kathleens on my list lives there."

Devlin stood, too. His expression didn't suggest that he'd caught her blunder, and she breathed a sigh of relief for small miracles.

"It's only eight, Laura," he said. "Usually the guests gather in the drawing room for Irish coffee and conversation after dinner. I thought you'd like to—"

"Maybe some other time," she cut in, with a forced smile, needing to get away, needing to regain a detached perspective on everything—on why she was here in Ireland, and why she mustn't spend any more time with this man than she already had. She reminded herself why she'd vowed not to get her heart tangled up in response to another man's sexy gaze. She must be practical and realistic—this time.

She forced herself to recall Vincent's look of disgust just before he'd deserted her and their baby daughter, and to remember the pity and guilt in Matt's eyes when he'd turned and walked away for the last time. Those painful memories hardened her resolve. "Have a nice vacation, Devlin," she trilled in a mock-cheerful tone. Dragging her gaze from the fire-lit planes of his face, she spun away.

"May I walk you to your room?" he asked. "That ladder isn't—"

"No! Don't bother," she objected over her shoulder, fairly racing to escape.

Frowning, Devlin watched her go. Everything that was male in him wanted to follow her, to take her in his arms and kiss the hell out of her. To kiss her until she sobbed, for he had a feeling she would—one day. Laura Todd would sob with joy when the right man kissed her—made love to her. Devlin knew in the depths of his soul who that right man would be. He had a hot stirring in his gut when he thought about it. He'd had the same stirring when he'd first seen her; then, when he'd held her in his arms rescuing her from the ladder; and afterward, when he'd risked asking her if she believed in love at first sight. He hadn't realized quite what the feeling had been at first. Maybe because his life had sunk into the lowest pit of hell, he hadn't expected a glimpse of heaven. But the truth had come to him with a blinding suddenness in her loft this afternoon: He loved Laura Todd.

She'd reacted strongly to his question about love at first sight. So strongly he knew she was resisting the idea with every fiber of her being. That's why he hadn't pursued it. Someday, though—someday soon—he would have to.

But for now, he didn't go after her. He could see that, for all her womanly need, she would violently protest any overt act of love—assuming that it was merely lust. Her feelings were damn clear when she'd gone ballistic after he'd made the idle remark about kinky fantasies. His only excuse was, he felt an intimacy for her she wasn't ready for, and he'd spoken without thinking. But he loved her, dammit. He loved her and hungered to know her fantasies—ached to help act them out with her and bring her to the brink of ecstasy. The problem was, how to convince Laura his desires weren't selfish and base.

Laura—his Laura—was a mystery. She was direct and outspoken on the surface. But for all her apparent forthrightness, she was keeping him at a distance. He was sure she wasn't like that with everyone. Only with aggressive men, for some reason. It was possible that men made her feel vulnerable in some way—especially men she was tempted by.

Devlin sat back and closed his eyes, not sure if he was happy about that or not. She was tempted by him, he knew. Her Freudian slip with the word *sex* hadn't gotten by him. But he'd known she'd go defensive and retreat even further if he called her on it. And she'd have denied it until Ireland shriveled up and blew away, if he'd dared to argue the point. But he knew in his gut that Laura was as turned-on by him as he was by her. All evening he'd seen interest, along with dread, in her eyes. Clearly, some man, or men, in her past had disappointed her cruelly. So, being attracted to Devlin, she would fight against it, not wanting to be hurt again.

How ironic. At thirty-five, he'd fallen into the deepest, ugliest, sewage-filled trench in his life. He'd lost his edge, didn't trust, and didn't know which way to turn. But in that vast, reeking darkness, he'd stumbled upon the finest gift a man could hope for—the woman who was meant for him. He knew that about Laura as clearly as his father had known it about his mother, on that day forty years ago. Duff Rafferty, a middle-aged Gaelic history teacher at the University of Chicago, had seen Claire Morton, a sophomore, sitting in the front row of his class, and he'd known. How many times had Devlin heard that story from his parents?

Their love had been sparked at first sight. Even though there had been twenty years' difference in their ages, Duff and Claire had been a devoted couple—and the three of them, the perfect family. And Devlin had always known that one day he would find his wife in just the same way. It was crazy, but considering his cynicism about most things, love was the one area of his life where Devlin remained an idealist. And it seemed to have paid off for him today.

He'd met Laura, a lovely woman on a noble quest— to give some unsuspecting Irish peasant a fortune. It was as though she'd been sent to him as a double miracle—to be his life's partner and to give him a renewed hope that good and right really could win out. His father would have laughed happily and said, "Devlin, my boy, on this day Irish angels smiled on you, and you've been granted a gift from the leprechauns more valuable than any pot of gold."

Devlin touched the silver chain at his neck. Now, all he had to do was convince Laura she need not fear him, that his love would make right whatever had gone wrong for her in the past. But first, he had to gain her trust. He could think of no better way than to persuade her to let him help her find Kathleen's poor bastard child. He needed—once more—to experience what it was like to do good for no other reason than the desire to help someone who'd been wronged.

Laura and her quest had caused something to flicker feebly back to life in Devlin's soul, and he planned to fight like hell to keep that flame from going dark and dead, again.

Unfortunately for his plan, Laura really believed she wanted *never* to see him again.

With a weary exhale, he got up, vowing that no matter how adamantly she might resist the idea, he would have to make sure she didn't get her way. Future Rafferty generations depended on it.

LAURA HOPPED ALONG THE gravel road toward the main highway, attempting to jostle her shoe onto her foot. She was late, and that was unlike her. Finally managing to push on the loafer, she accelerated into a dead run, praying the bus would be just a little late, too.

She couldn't remember when she'd had such rotten luck. First her alarm hadn't worked, causing her to miss breakfast. That probably wasn't so bad, since she might have seen Devlin in there, and she really didn't think seeing him was a good idea. He'd spent half the night crashing into her dreams, anyway.

She forced that thought from her mind. She had enough troubles already. First of all, she'd had one heck of a time finding the shoe she'd just shoved on her foot. She was positive that she'd looked under the bed three times, then suddenly there it was. It was almost as though it had been playing a game of hide-and-seek with her. She supposed she could have worn another pair but the loafers were her most comfortable. Besides, her only other comfortable shoes were sandals. With the heavy mist shrouding the countryside, she had no intention of catching pneumonia by going practically barefoot in fifty-degree weather.

So, here she was, starving to death, sprinting through the dank, early-morning fog, and hoping she wouldn't have to wait four hours for her next chance to get to

Dingle. "Please, let the seven o'clock bus be late, too!" she wheezed.

She checked her watch, squinting at it. There was a cloudiness behind the crystal. "Oh, no," she moaned. "How did it get wet?" That was the end of knowing what time it was. What a gruesome first day this was turning out to be!

At last finding herself at the main road, she plunked down on the rough wooden bench to wait. Every time a motor growled in the distance, she jumped up. Each time, whatever that motor had been attached to, zoomed on by. There were no buses.

Then, a hard rain began to fall. Her unlined wool coat soaked up the moisture like a thirsty camel and her hair, soon plastered to her head in straggly strands, gave lie to the bold red letters on her hair-spray can that promised "extra-hold even in a thundershower." It was obvious she'd missed the bus. Since she had no intention of waiting hours for the next one in the pouring rain, she began her soggy trek back to her loft room.

She was so absorbed in her misery, she didn't hear the car engine. A light blue British compact crawled to a stop beside her on the gravel drive.

She paused and peered at it as someone leaned across to her side and began to roll down the window. When it was cranked low enough, Laura was horrified to discover Devlin sitting there. Why she cared that he would be the one human in the world out in weather like this to witness her impersonation of a sopping rodent, she couldn't fathom. Suddenly she had an urge to lurch off into the curtain of rain and become sucked into one of those famous Irish bogs she'd heard about. But that would be chickenhearted, she supposed. So, with shivering bravado, she said, "Nothing like a brisk walk in the morning t-to open your pores."

"I'd suggest you not open them too much or you'll drown."

She ran a hand through her dripping hair and began to march forward. Maybe if she ignored him he'd go away.

It didn't work. He continued to move slowly forward, keeping pace with her. After a few seconds, he shouted, "I missed the bus this morning."

"What were you going to do, store that car under the seat?"

A smile tugged at the corners of his mouth. "Actually, I was looking for you. I drove to Dingle, but didn't see you there."

"I can't imagine why."

He didn't say anything for a minute—just crept along, keeping up with her labored trudging. After she'd moved about twenty feet, he said, "I'm sorry I missed you. Too bad whoever gave you a ride back couldn't have brought you all the way. How'd it go? Are you returning in triumph?"

She clamped her lips together. Why couldn't he simply drive on by and leave her alone in her misery. *Triumph?* She hadn't even triumphed enough to catch a lousy bus! But how could she admit that, now? She'd already let him think she'd been to Dingle and back.

What was her problem with this man? If it had been anyone else she'd met at the hotel, she'd have asked if she could get in out of the rain, but, no. She was acting like a ninny—freezing, stumbling along in ruined shoes, and lying for no good reason. And for what?

Why couldn't she confess that she'd missed the bus and ask for a ride home? What was it about this man that short-circuited her brain and made her lose her good sense? Could she really be so tempted by him that a few measly seconds of sitting close to him in a compact car could put her sound, well-thought-out plans where men were concerned in jeopardy? Now that was really crazy!

"Laura!" he called. "Did you hear me?"

Confused and trapped, she whirled on him. "Right! Sure! I heard you. And, yes, I'm the *picture* of triumph. Now, go away while I exult in the rain, by myself. It's a little ceremony I invented—I like to call it my-triumph-in-the-rain-dance. I'm afraid it's secret and sacred and if you witnessed it I'd have to kill you—"

"You missed the bus, didn't you," he interrupted.

She stilled, staring daggers at him. "You knew! And you let me—let me—"

He opened the car door nearest her, finishing, "Make a fool of yourself? I hadn't planned on it, but it wouldn't take Sherlock Holmes to guess what happened." He shook his head at her. "Besides, I caught up with the bus about a half mile out of Dingle where it'd had a flat. I thought you might be on it so I asked the driver. He said he didn't pick up any Americans this morning." Nodding toward the passenger seat, he ordered softly, "Get in."

Humiliated, she went rigid. "You were following me?"

"I was looking for you." He patted the seat. "Come on. You're soaked."

Mortified that she managed to continually make a fool of herself in front of this man—or even worse, *because* of him—she snapped defiantly, "I wouldn't get into a car with you now if you got down on all fours and bayed at the moon!"

He moved away from the window, disappearing from her view. *Finally!* He was going to leave her alone. She felt an odd twinge, but didn't have time to analyze it. An instant later a car door slammed. Her head jerked up to see Devlin coming around the front of his car toward her. When he reached her side, he pulled the passenger door wide and declared, "You're the most stubborn woman I've ever had the misfortune to meet. Get in the damned car!"

He left her little choice in the matter. Against her will, she found herself deposited on the passenger seat. Too shocked to react, she could only sprawl there while he sprinted back around the car and climbed in behind the wheel.

His dark hair was spangled with raindrops and his bomber jacket glistened. She had the wayward thought that he'd probably *never* look waterlogged, even drenched to the skin. He'd no doubt simply look—uh—well lubricated. She flinched at her turn of mind. Apparently, sleeping alone was wearing on her more than she'd realized.

"Look, Laura," he began, once he was seated. "I started out this morning wanting to help you—"

"Ha!" she scoffed, steeling herself against his allure. "That's a likely—"

"When I caught up with you," he cut in, "and you insisted on pretending you were crazy about being drenched, I went along. But hell, I didn't think your pride would force you to keep up the charade forever." He exhaled tiredly. "A 'triumph-in-the-rain-dance,' for Pete's sake. Do I look like that much of an idiot?"

She boldly returned his stare, her narrowed gaze clashing with his.

"Never mind," he muttered. "I'm no masochist."

She crossed her arms before her and focused straight ahead, her animosity a living breathing entity in the confines of the car. After another minute of tense silence, she was startled to hear him chuckle.

"That pride of yours is going to do you in one day if you're not careful," he cautioned.

She shifted away, still irked, though worried that he might be on to something. She did have a lot of pride—sometimes foolish, perhaps. Like now, when she'd insisted on walking in a cold rain and setting herself up for a case of pneumonia so she could sicken and die in a foreign country. That was high-tech stupid!

But maybe it wasn't simply pride at work here. Devlin had a strange effect on her—a frightening one. Maybe what looked like foolish pride to him was, to some extent, her defense system kicking in—a kind of verbal stiff-arm—to ward off a dangerous attraction. She'd learned the hard way, to be wary of coaxing words and handsome faces.

But she was only human. She wanted what everybody wanted—to love and be loved. But not at all costs. It was too bad that what often passed for love faded when unattractive strings were attached. Laura wasn't sure she would ever heal from her past hurts, so she'd prudently adapted a thorny manner when confronted by Devlin's charisma. Let him assume it was foolish pride if he wished. It would be simpler that way.

"Well, Mr. Rafferty," she ground out, struggling to put distance between them. "What about your warped code of gallantry? Throwing women into cars won't win you any Nobel Peace prizes!"

"Hell. And I thought that was the way Gandhi got his."

She winced, only just becoming aware that they were in motion. "I—er—I think I'll crawl into the back and crouch on the floorboards. I have a problem with being on the wrong side of a car on the wrong side of the road."

"We've only got a few hundred feet to go," he said. "You're going to have to get a grip if you intend to get around in this country."

"That won't be necessary. I intend to find Kathleen at noon, give her the good news and get back to the States where people drive correctly."

"I'm sure the Irish drive this way with the sole purpose of irritating American tourists."

She passed him a mutinous look but said nothing.

"By the way," Devlin remarked, "I thought you said you had *three* Kathleens on your list."

"This Kathleen could be the right one. I may not have to look further."

"What if she's not?"

"That's right. Be negative."

He pulled the car to a stop in front of the gatehouse before facing her. "Answer my question, dammit. What if she's not the right Kathleen?"

Laura considered her fists, clenched in her lap. "Then I'll have to go to Bangor, I suppose."

"By bus?"

"Of course. They run there—" concern edging her voice, she looked up "—don't they?" She hadn't considered the possibility that she might not be able to get to the tiny hamlet by bus.

He nodded. "Ireland has a very nice bus system." After a pause, he tossed her a meaningful look. "If you can catch one, that is."

Even an unconscious person couldn't have missed his mockery. Her temper flaring, Laura fumbled with the door handle but he halted her, taking hold of her shoulder.

"Bad joke. I only meant, if you let me drive you—"

"Not on your life. I wouldn't go anywhere with you if you had the only transportation in the Northern hemisphere!"

"Laura," he murmured near her ear. "I want to help you. I *need* to. . . ."

No matter how hard she tried, she couldn't resist the melancholy note in his voice. Her anger dissipated, though her mind cried out a warning that she shouldn't be near this man. Shouldn't listen to him, now. He pushed buttons she didn't want pushed, brought to life longings she didn't dare encourage.

She turned toward Devlin. His gaze was kindled with a need so earnest it took away her breath. He was waiting for her answer, and that answer was desperately important to him.

Somehow, Laura sensed that if she said yes—if she let Devlin help her—his inner pain would begin to heal. How could any right-thinking person say no?

His unwavering stare disturbed her, but also filled her with a thrilling expectancy. Those eyes, beautifully blue and shimmering with unspoken torment, were striking in their mute appeal. Undeniable. She wavered, knowing what she should do—for her own good—but . . .

"Please . . ." he whispered.

Dismay flooded through her. That one word, spoken with such powerful urgency, crumbled the last of her resolve. She wasn't sure which motive finally won out—the desire to help a fellow human being in pain, or the longing to be close to one extremely magnetic man....

She tugged loose from his grasp and scrambled out of the car. Before racing for her door, she ducked back inside the car. "Okay, okay. If you're set on doing this, pick me up here in an hour. I'm *sure* we'll be done by noon, anyway."

Devlin's eyes widened slightly, his surprise genuine. He shifted, and Laura suspected he planned to squeeze her hand in thanks. From the little he'd said, she figured he was from one of those touchy-huggy-kissy families, and the gesture would mean little to him. But Laura hadn't been raised that way. To her, a touch between a man and a woman was an intimate act, to be taken seriously. She didn't appreciate having her space casually invaded. And she had a worrisome suspicion that once Devlin Rafferty invaded a woman's space—casually or otherwise—it stayed invaded. Avoiding his touch, she ducked out of the car and slammed the door, making it unmistakable where they stood: business—first, last and always.

3

Laura took a last dismal look at herself in her bathroom mirror. Her hair was frizzy around the edges. She didn't know what she might have done differently to get her hair dryer to work properly. All she'd managed to achieve was a little lukewarm air seepage—not enough to cause an actual breeze, just enough to frustrate her to the brink of screaming. Apparently her gatehouse room's electricity supply was capricious, to say the least.

As a last resort, she'd ended up crouched before the fire, fluffing her brand-new perm to get it dry, and in the process, toasting her head. She was afraid her hairdresser had been optimistic when she'd announced, "This cut will be simple to work with." Laura could almost cry. Not even her beautician would have envisioned trying to get this "simple-to-work-with" mess to fall obligingly into place while being barbecued over a roaring peat fire.

So she looked a little singed. *So what!* She drew in a deep, calming breath.

Her main problem was her coat. Even after hanging on the back of a chair near the heat of the fire, the wool was still too clammy to wear. Dejected, she slipped on a tunic-length, carpet-pattern sweater—the warmest thing she had. Wine, gold and black, it went with her ebony stirrup pants. She'd dug out a not-too-comfy pair of ankle boots. Even if they caused blisters, she was darned if she'd be cold again today! Hearing a knock, she stilled. It had to be Devlin. Right on time, according to the travel alarm next to her bed.

"You decent?" he asked, after cracking open the door.

She grabbed her purse. "I'm coming."

He climbed halfway up, all the while inspecting her with interest. She froze, her breathing becoming labored at his steadied, silent inspection. He was still wearing his bomber jacket and jeans, but looking freshly combed and all too sexy.

Though he made no move to speak, his mouth twisted wryly. Swallowing, she tried not to care that he was clearly amused by her Little Orphan Annie look.

Unwilling to be the source of his perverse amusement one second longer, she forced a smile. "I know how it is," she quipped, sarcasm in her tone. "Some days you find yourself on a ladder and forget if you're going up or down. Happens to my great-uncle Snapper all the time. Of course, he lives in a—shall we say— *guarded* environment? Why don't you try going down?"

Compressing his lips, plainly masking a grin, he lifted a hand. "Would you like some help?"

She tossed him her handbag. "This'll help. Thanks."

He got her message, and backed down the ladder, allowing her to descend on her own. When they reached the door and he was holding it open, she took the bag back and eyed him dubiously. "Okay. Get it off your chest. I look like a comic-book character. I know it. Make your crack and get it over with."

"I didn't say anything," he responded, his face a bit too straight to be believed. Then, turning to indicate the slate-gray sky, he commented, "It's not raining anymore."

She glanced around the puddle-dotted courtyard. It was true. "Thank goodness for that," she remarked.

"I brought an umbrella, just in case."

"Er—thanks," she mumbled, trudging toward the car.

When she reached the door, he called, "You're going to drive?"

She peered at him over her shoulder. "What would make you think an absurd thing like that?"

"Maybe the fact that you're about to get in on the driver's side."

She looked in the window. Sure enough, there it was: a steering wheel. Feeling like a fool, she picked her way around puddles to the other door.

"It wouldn't hurt you to do some driving while you're here," he suggested. "What if you have to come back to the British Isles on business and I'm not available to drive you?"

"I'd have a huge party," she muttered as she climbed in.

He slid behind the wheel and looked at her askance. "I heard that, Mrs. Todd," he chided. "Would it kill you to try to be friends? I mean, since we'll be traveling around Ireland together?"

She faced him. He was right, of course—though she was confident they wouldn't be traveling far or for long. Technically, he was doing her a big favor, even if allowing him to do it was against her better judgment. She decided to relent, and with a distracted nod, agreed, "All right. But I'm paying for the gas."

His brows drew together. "Gas isn't cheap."

"Nevertheless, I'm paying. I'm the one with an expense account—and a job," she argued.

He made no comment, but Laura noted the bleak shadow that passed over his face at the reminder of whatever it was that had torn up his world.

She felt rotten for being responsible for the unhappy recollection. "Er—I'm sorry about snapping at you before," she confessed, deciding he deserved better than she'd been giving him. It wasn't his fault that he made her tingle when he walked into a room. Besides, she had to admit that being driven around would make her job more efficient than trying to catch buses. She'd already discovered *that* could be a royal pain. "It's probably jet lag—and nervousness," she continued, only partly fibbing. She really was nervous, and not just because of the bothersome way he stirred her emotions. This assignment was the biggest opportunity she'd been given in her eight years with the Abandoned Property Division. Truthfully, she told him, "Finding Josh Kincade's heir is important to me. I guess I'm a little on edge about that."

Suddenly his solemn expression eased as his lips quirked into a half grin. The expression was almost genuine—almost, although there was still the persistent darkness lurking in his eyes. "You'll find Kathleen, Laura," he offered encouragingly.

She experienced a little shiver along her spine at his assurance and found herself softening toward him.

"Friends?" he asked, extending a hand toward her.

Her gaze darted from his outstretched fingers to his face, unable to resist another peek at his generous mouth, aquiline nose and drop-dead blue eyes. There was something very seductive about the way he was watching her, though she had the feeling he was unaware of it. Without being quite mindful of what she was doing, she lifted her hand toward his. "Friends," she echoed, then found herself adding, "And—uh—did I ever say thanks for the lift?" How thoughtless of her to have let it go this long, not telling him she appreciated his offer to help.

"Let's say we're giving each other a lift," he replied, his fingers engulfing hers. As soon as her hand was wrapped in his, something hot sizzled between them like an electrical surge, making her go weak. She had a self-protective impulse to pull away and bolt from the car, but she fought it. Surely it was her overwrought imagination, the result of her half-broiled brains. She'd made enough of a fool of herself in front of this man, so there would be no car-bolting. He was just a good-looking man, and *they* were a dime a dozen. Withdrawing her fingers in what she trusted was a casual manner, she planted them in her lap, twisting them in her other hand. "Let's go," she managed, her tone breathy.

He started the engine and steered them toward the fishing village of Dingle and—Laura hoped desperately—toward the *right* Kathleen.

As they pulled onto the winding seacoast road, she flicked a discreet glance at his profile, wondering if their contact had unnerved him the way it had her. However, his expression was unreadable.

THE INTERIOR OF THE CAR was pleasantly warm, and the radio station Devlin had chosen was playing Irish folk music performed by an interesting combination of harp and violin. The mellow tunes soothed her. She stared out the window at the rugged wild beauty of the fjord coast of Dingle Bay. It would have been a magnificent experience, but for the fact that cars kept zooming by on what Laura felt to be the wrong side of the road, continually jarring her out of her sight-seeing mood.

In an effort to keep from gasping with every car that careened by during the twenty-minute drive, Laura forced herself to sit back. She stared out the window. The sea looked troubled. She knew exactly how it felt.

"Laura," he coaxed, breaking the long silence. "How did you find your three Kathleens?"

"I wrote to Quillan Phelan last month. Though he and his wife only bought the place ten years ago, he kept the old records and went through them. They were sketchy, but he managed to find three possibles. It took me a while to track down their current addresses, but I did. One lives in Dingle. One moved several times but I found her in Bangor, and the third is in Dublin. It'll be delicate getting the right Kathleen to admit to giving birth to an illegitimate child." She peered over at him. "I'll do the talking. I know how to be delicate."

He gave her a narrowed glance. "What makes you think I can't be delicate?"

She rolled her eyes. "This, from a man who throws women into cars?"

A provoking smile tugged at his mouth.

"You stay in the car," Laura ordered.

"Spoilsport," he objected, his tone more kidding than offended.

Laura had a sinking feeling she'd have a tough time keeping Devlin Rafferty in any car if he had an urge to get out. She had a wild thought and ran over it in her brain. *Say, Devlin, would you mind stepping into the trunk for a minute? I think I lost a button, way, way in the back.* Then, when he climbed in, she could slam down the lid and— No. He'd never fall for that. Besides, she doubted if a man over six feet tall would even fit in such a tiny trunk. Running a hand through the tangle of curls at her temple, she exhaled wearily, hoping her job in Ireland was almost over. She'd only been here twenty-four hours and already her nerves were in shreds. She wondered if foreign travel affected everyone this way.

"Dingle's up ahead," Devlin announced. "What's the address?"

She looked up and caught sight of an array of colorful fishing boats docked in the quaint little harbor. So, this was Dingle. Well, she wasn't here to sightsee. Rummaging in her bag for her notebook, she concentrated on the job at hand. "Hawthorn Cottage, number 7, Killybeggs Road. The McMahon residence."

"Check."

"You are going to be *good*, aren't you?"

"I can only do my best," he said, with a wicked grin.

Laura shook her head, exasperated. "Seriously, can you be *circumspect* or must I insist that you remain in the car?"

"I resent that," he countered, with mock affront. "Circumspect is my middle name."

"Oh, I don't know, Devlin," she replied uneasily. "I'm having second thoughts about this. You're pushy, smart-mouthed, and you've got a lawyer's argumentativeness. You could screw things up."

"Careful," he warned. "A man could collapse under the weight of such flattery."

He'd spoken quietly, and seemed to have drifted nearer. Suddenly the car felt too warm. Laura shifted restively in her seat. Devlin loomed, broad-shouldered and virile. The force of his sexual magnetism dazed her as he drew closer and closer. She was transfixed by deliciously appealing lips—lips that were moving ever nearer to hers.

There was the piercing honk of a distant car, and even in her dazed state, Laura was aware that they'd come to a stop.

"Are we—there?" she whispered.

He gradually drew away, those sexy lips curving in a rueful grin. "It's just a hunch," he said huskily, "but I'd say we were damned close."

KATHLEEN MCMAHON WAS a pleasant, stubby woman with a wide, thin-lipped smile and an ample scattering of freckles on her face. Though in her late fifties by Laura's estimation, she had fine, brown hair without a streak of gray. All bustle and curiosity, Kathleen invited them in. "Mind, I'll not be takin' no for an answer. You'll have tea, at least, after your drive," she insisted, wiping her hands on her apron. "Me Mick, the ignorant old fool," she said with a shy smile, "he only just rang me up from the pub ta say you was comin' late." She poked a stray wisp of hair back into the bun at her nape, and giggled, "I rue the day I ever walked out with that thick. Mind, himself has been a good provider, but he's never had a head for rememberin' messages—these thirty-odd years." She indicated the bubbling iron kettle on the stove opposite the soot-stained fireplace, urging, "Go along with ya to the sofa. I'll just be a minute."

Laura scanned the place. It was the first Irish cottage she'd ever seen. The walls in the main room of the house were constructed of rough stone and timber. There was an antique wag-on-the-wall clock between two deep-set windows on the seaward side of the cottage, and a battered brass bed warmer leaned against the hearth.

Lace curtains fluttered in a sea breeze, and goatskin rugs were scattered about the wood floor. Kathleen lifted a hand and repeated her urging, "Sit ye, now. I'll just be a minute."

Laura didn't have the heart to object to all the work Kathleen was going to. It was clear that the woman was excited to have mysterious American visitors in her little cottage. As Kathleen prepared the tea, Laura moved to the pine sofa. Its cushions were covered in a printed cotton that mimicked ivy vines. A small round table beside the couch was covered with a red-checked horse blanket. On it sat a ginger jar containing a bright mix of local flowers. One half of a wooden barrel served as a coffee table between the sofa and two old pine chairs, their seats and backs covered in the same green-and-white cotton as the sofa.

Laura gave Devlin a narrowed look, trying to squeeze minimal obedience from him. However, he merely smiled and continued to wander about the room, admiring the McMahons' possessions.

"I'm *that* curious to know what business brought ye all this way ta me door from America," Kathleen twittered as she carried in a tea tray heaped with meringues. After placing the tray on the coffee table, she looked over at Devlin, who was holding a framed picture. "Ya say, the likes o' him is yer assistant?"

Laura felt a little badly about the deception, but nodded.

"Now, ain't that grand." She offered Laura a cup of her steaming black brew. Lowering her voice, she observed, "He has shoulders on 'im like an ox."

Laura blanched, sipping the strong concoction to keep from having to comment. She glanced at Devlin.

He didn't seem to be listening to them, but the room was so small, she knew he had to have heard.

"Mrs. McMahon," Laura began, working at broaching a difficult subject, "Mr. Rafferty and I are here, because—"

"Rafferty, ye say?" she broke in, her expression becoming animated. "Could it be that I know yer people, Mr. Rafferty? Murphy O'Rourke Rafferty of Athlone in County Westmeath?"

Devlin set the photograph down. "Could be distant cousins. My grandfather was from County Westmeath. But he immigrated to America in the thirties."

Kathleen clasped her hands together. "The saints preserve us, why, lad, me cousin Sean O'Dea married Murphy's daughter, Keely. I'd wager we're kissin' kin."

Devlin smiled at the older woman, and though the look wasn't aimed her way, Laura felt a melting effect.

Evidently, the calculated charm wasn't lost on Kathleen, for she giggled, whispering to Laura, "'Tis a bold man, yer Mr. Rafferty. I'm thinkin' he'd make a fine husband for some lucky colleen."

Laura cleared her throat, not daring to look in Devlin's direction. She only hoped he'd missed the murmured praise. "Yes—well, Mrs. McMahon, perhaps we should get back to why I'm here."

"Excuse me—Ms. Todd?" Devlin interrupted.

Disconcerted by the continued interruptions, she glanced sharply his way. "Can't it wait—Mr. Rafferty?"

"It could," he offered with an inclination of his head. "But I think you should step over here for a moment."

With gritted teeth, she replaced her cup on its saucer and rose. "Pardon me one moment, Mrs. McMahon?"

The portly woman nodded, taking up her own cup and sipping.

When Laura reached Devlin's side, she hissed, "What is it? I've hardly had a chance to get a word in edgewise with the two of you gabbing and flirting!"

Devlin's chuckle was deep. "Why, Laura, are you jealous?"

"I won't dignify that with an answer," she ground out. "What was so all-fired important, anyway?"

He indicated the photo with a subtle nod of his head. "Take a good look at that."

She glared at it. Before her she saw what was obviously a recent McMahon family portrait. Captured there was a tall, thin man with buckteeth, a bulbous Adam's apple, and a nose that could have doubled for an avocado. He was the homeliest man Laura could ever recall seeing. His hair was bright red, and his eyes were narrow slits in a gaunt, pointy face.

As her inspection moved from person to person, Laura became aware that the four younger McMahons, two boys and two girls, resembled the man in almost comical exactness, except for the youngest, who bore his mother's thick field of freckles across his avocado-like snout.

Laura realized what Devlin had been trying to say, and picked up the framed photograph. Carrying it back to the sofa, she handed it to Kathleen, remarking, "You have a handsome family, Mrs. McMahon. Are these all of your children?"

Kathleen smiled indulgently. "Oh my, yes." Pointing proudly, she said, "There be me eldest—a mother's pride and joy—me Michael. He's a priest over in Dublin, and I don't mind sayin', a fine, God-fearin' lad."

Laura held her breath as Kathleen went on to list the names of her other three children. When she'd finished, Devlin smiled that charming smile and said, "Why, Mrs. McMahon. You don't look old enough to have a son so strapping and fine as Michael. May I ask his age?"

Kathleen flushed beneath the blanket of freckles and touched the image of her homely boy with reverence. "Oh, 'tis ashamed ye should be, Mr. Rafferty, tease that ye are. Me Michael turns all o' thirty-six, come June."

Laura sank back, deflated. First of all, there was no way Kathleen McMahon could have had another child before Michael and still fit the time period for Josh Kincade to have fathered a child of hers. Second, there was no chance that Michael was *not* the offspring of the homely man pictured there with his arm slung about the spindly shoulders of his bucktoothed firstborn.

"Now," Kathleen asked, picking up a teacup and pastry and offering them to Devlin. "What was it ye wanted to speak with me about that brought you all this far way?"

As he took a seat on one of the pine chairs opposite the women, he said, "Our questions concern a time long ago, when you worked as a housemaid at the Dingle Bay Country House Hotel."

Laura stared at him, confused. What was he going to say? As it stood, they had no business at all with this Kathleen, now. They might as well leave and move on down their list of Kathleens.

"Yes," the woman agreed, nodding. "'Twas many years ago. Grand old place. It is still."

"You see, Kathleen . . ." He paused, gracing her with a heart-stopping smile. "May I call you Kathleen?"

She blushed. "Sure, and bless ya for bein' a gentleman."

Laura coughed into her linen napkin to get his attention and warn him off, but he didn't indicate that he was aware she was even in the room.

"Our mission concerns the ugly specter of devil demons, Kathleen," he said, his expression serious, as he leaned forward and spoke in hushed tones.

"D-devil demons?" Kathleen echoed, her brown eyes widening in fear.

Devlin nodded. "We're doing paranormal research in suspected haunted castles and great houses of Ireland, and we've heard some ghastly tales about the Dingle Bay hotel. Specifically during the time you worked there. We hoped, perhaps you'd witnessed something demonic back then that we might document for our book—*Hell on Earth*."

Laura's lips parted in astonishment at his outlandish lie. She shot a glimpse at Kathleen. The woman had stood abruptly, apprehension on her face. "I—no! There be no devil demons at Dingle Bay!" she whispered, clutching her hands to her breasts. 'Tis a thought to shun." Agitated, she stuttered, "See'n as—as how I'm a God-fearin' woman, you can be savin' yer breath talkin' the likes o' that in me home."

"I assure you," Laura said kindly, wanting to allay the woman's fears, "we—we mean no harm." She passed Devlin an I-can't-believe-you-got-us-into-this glare, adding "We'll just be—going...."

Crossing herself, Kathleen turned a jaundiced eye on Laura and scolded, "If I be ye, me girl, I'd be lookin' to give some good man a nice home and chicks, not out chasin' devil spirits." Wagging a finger, she cautioned, "And, I'd be takin' shears to that poor mess o' curls.

You'll never catch a man with hair the likes o' wool on a sickly lamb."

Devlin's strangled chuckle was impossible to miss, though to Kathleen it must have sounded like a cough. "Bless ye, me boy," she said, regarding him with a measure of forgiveness. Probably because they were related—at least in her mind.

Solemnly, Kathleen added, "There's many that knows that fine old hotel, and none who'd speak a word against it. Hellish ghouls, indeed!"

Laura felt a hand at her elbow. "I think, then, Kathleen," Devlin was saying as he dragged Laura to her feet, "we've been badly misinformed. Sorry to have bothered you."

The Irishwoman waddled after them. "Now, I didn't say the grand old place was without its mischief," she admitted, her injured tone suddenly gone.

"How so?" Devlin asked as they reached the door.

Kathleen's lips curved upward at some memory. "Oh, I did see me share of fun, that I did. Most in the gatehouse loft, it was."

Laura blinked, startled at the mention of her room.

Kathleen giggled. "Seems the little people had a special likin' for playin' tricks on them who tarried there. Like takin' liberties with a person's belongin's, hidin' 'em in plain sight." Her shoulders shook as she tittered at the thought. "Mind, myself, I never saw a thing, but too many times, I was called in to look for a shoe that was sittin'—"

"Beneath the bottom-right corner of the bed?" Laura finished for her, strangely aware she would be right, but wishing she were wrong.

Kathleen gaped. "Why—sure, and how did ye know that?" she asked, astonished.

Devlin cleared his throat, getting their attention. "I think we'd better be going now, Kathleen. Thank you for your kind hospitality."

Kathleen shook his hand, then blushed as she closed the door at their departure.

Once back in the car, Laura settled against the seat, disappointed and tense. Devlin started the engine, then shifted his wide shoulders in such a way that she was positive he was watching her. Not sure why, she hesitated to meet his gaze.

"Laura," he said, softly. "I know you're unhappy, and I'm sorry it wasn't this Kathleen."

She allowed herself an audible sigh.

"What now?" he asked, and she was aware that he was still regarding her closely.

Needing something to do, she rummaged in her purse and pulled out the notebook, scanning the data she'd collected. "Kathleen Smythe, in Bangor, is next on my list."

"Bangor it is," he said, starting the engine.

"But—" She swiveled to face him. "Bangor's way north of here. I can't ask you to take me all that way."

"I'd better go along. You're not fast enough on your feet. What excuse would you have come up with to get out of there?"

His playful rebuke reminded her of his devil-demon fabrication, and she frowned at him. "Oh, that was brilliant. Whatever made you come up with such a crazy excuse?"

"Don't know." He shrugged. "Maybe because I watched *The Amityville Horror* on the late-night movie just before I left Chicago."

"Fine," she muttered. "Thanks to your grotesque taste in movies, Kathleen stared at me like she thought my head was going to start spinning around on my neck. Any second, I thought she'd run screaming for an exorcist!"

He chuckled. "Not a chance. Remember, she thinks I'm her cousin."

"Everybody in Ireland can't be tricked into believing they're related to a Rafferty," she replied. "You'll get us in trouble, yet."

"Speaking of that," he said. "I gather you had some trouble locating a shoe this morning."

"Don't start babbling about little people to me again," she retorted indignantly. "That was just a coincidence."

"Laura," he said, his voice dropping a notch, "before you leave Ireland, you'll believe."

"In leprechauns?" she scoffed. "Don't be ridiculous."

His unsettling smile was cryptic and his lazy-lidded eyes unreadable as he turned away to shift into gear.

They headed out of Dingle in silence. As Laura stared unseeing out her window, an unease invaded her body. She couldn't be sure—and there was every possibility she was wrong—but she'd had the strangest feeling, a minute ago, that Devlin hadn't been talking about *leprechauns* at all....

4

LAURA WISHED SHE COULD be teleported to Bangor and avoid this long drive with Devlin Rafferty. He was an exciting man whose rugged vitality drew her. She didn't need this sort of complication in her life, didn't want it. Had run from it for three years. Unfortunately, the deed was done, now. She'd said he could come, said he could help. She only hoped the whole ordeal would be over tonight. And the fact that Devlin was obviously happy with the planned trip only added to her discomfort.

"Did you get in touch with her?" he asked.

"I talked with her housekeeper. She said Kathleen Smythe will be available either late this afternoon or early evening."

"Her housekeeper?" he asked, curiosity in his tone. "Sounds like our second Kathleen's done pretty well."

Out of nervousness, Laura smoothed her hair back. "After she left Dingle Bay, she took a job as a nanny in an English home," she explained. "Three years later, she married one of the wealthy brothers. He's dead now, so she's moved back to Ireland."

"Think she had time in there to have Kincade's baby?"

Reluctantly Laura flicked him a glance, and her breath caught at what she saw. Those expressive blue eyes had a lethal appeal, and she was speechless. It took her several seconds to find her voice. "We'll—er—have to find that out, won't we?"

His look was frank, almost amused, as he lounged there against the door frame. "We?" he echoed. "Have you forgotten my *Amityville Horror* comment?"

She shrugged, assuming a nonchalance she didn't feel. "I may have overreacted. It got us out of there." After a long pause, and with the beginnings of a wry smile at the absurd memory, she admitted, "Besides, your pointing out that family portrait to me saved time and embarrassment."

He didn't speak, but she saw the gleam of satisfaction in his eyes. It occurred to her that he must have been waiting for a gracious remark, a compliment. She felt a surge of guilt, knowing she'd been pretty hard on him. But that couldn't be helped. She had no intention of slipping into bed with a virtual stranger simply because they felt a spark of attraction for each other, and, the terrible truth was, Devlin Rafferty was a handsome, tempting hunk of—

"Thanks, Laura," he murmured, breaking through her heated thoughts as he shifted into gear.

Motoring down Dingle Bay Country House's long drive, they headed northeast toward Tralee.

"You say Kathleen number two can see us late this afternoon?" he asked.

Relieved at the change of subject, Laura amended, "Or early evening."

"That should work out about right," he said. "We ought to get there in about four hours, give or take, even going the scenic route."

"What scenic route?" she asked almost accusingly. "I'm not being paid to sightsee."

"You don't give yourself much space, do you."

"Whatever 'space' I give myself is my business," she blurted. His reproof galled her, not because it wasn't his business, but because it was so depressingly on target. Nevertheless, she'd be darned if she'd admit that to him. He had no business butting into her personal affairs. She'd thought she'd made that clear this morning.

He said nothing more as he drove, seeming to concentrate on his driving. Without conscious thought or interest, she noted that they'd turned onto a long ribbon of winding country road. Devlin's car was gliding over wet pavement through a drizzle that transformed the countryside into a multitude of rich hues of green.

Laura was so agitated, she couldn't enjoy the peaceful scenery. Her hard-fought composure was fast seeping away. How could Devlin undo her so with one, softly spoken reprimand? She was tougher than that, for heaven's sake! Still, the naked truth of Devlin's words echoed over and over in her brain. *You don't give yourself much space, do you.* It hadn't been a question, but an uncalled-for insight, and she wouldn't forgive him for saying it—however true it might be.

"The scenic route isn't going to take that much longer, Laura," he said. "Relax and enjoy yourself for a change."

Her irritation mounted at his continued assumption that most of the time she was tense and uptight. She didn't appreciate his attitude—as though he knew what was best for her and to heck with what she might want!

"Look," she began, having had enough. "I'm very grateful for the ride, but if you insist on psychoanalyzing me all afternoon, I'll get out now and catch the first bus and you can go . . ." She paused, deciding not to go through with her first instinct to tell him to go to hell, and amended, "Take the scenic route—alone!"

"Would you rather talk about the mating habits of squirrels? There's a fun topic," he taunted, not in the least chastened by her reprimand. That fact galled her almost to distraction.

"I'm getting out of the car!" she warned. "Stop here or I'll jump!"

"I think you're bluffing."

"Well, the joke's on you, isn't it," she snapped, hoping he wouldn't really call her bluff. "I—I offered to let you come along, against my better judgment, and if you don't behave, I'll—I'll dump you and your car right here!"

He'd slowed down, and Laura had a sick feeling he was going to drop her off in the middle of nowhere. "Well?" she demanded, her heart pounding. "Are you going to behave, or do we part company here?"

"Are you having some sort of breakdown—maybe from lack of food or jet lag?"

"I most certainly am not!" In truth, she wasn't totally sure about that. This man seemed to make her go a little nutty every time he opened his mouth. "You'll know when I have a breakdown!" she retorted. "I'll probably do something really crazy—probably act like I'm fond of you!"

The corner of his mouth twisted wryly. "Don't go to any special trouble on my account."

"Oh, just drive," she spat out tiredly.

Without comment, he sped up, and she breathed a sigh of relief. Then she had an unsettling thought. Maybe he was purposely trying to hack her off just to have a little entertainment on the ride. Maybe this was his 'Let's see how mad we can make Laura' game! Lawyers played games like that. They cut their teeth on friendly debates. At least they probably *thought* they were friendly, harmless little discussions. When, to other people, they were more like knock-down-drag-out fights!

Laura had a friend, Betty, a lawyer. For years, in school, she'd driven Laura nuts with her incessant arguing about everything. She'd have argued that the sun was up even if it was pitch-black outside. And she probably could have convinced people she was right. Today Betty was a successful criminal lawyer in Miami. But she still didn't know how to just *talk* to people. She was possessed with the need to prove her point. It was an exhausting friendship, to say the least.

But Betty had a good heart, bless her pointed little head! And that propensity to tick people off was what made her the ace she was at cross-examining witnesses—able to smile in the face of stark, unadulterated hatred.

Laura couldn't fault lawyers for their argumentative approach to life, but she didn't have to adore it or seek out such personalities. And she sure didn't plan to give Devlin the entertainment at her expense he was angling for. She'd beat him at his game by being so pleasant and so sickeningly agreeable it would make Mr. Rogers barf all over his neighborhood. Devlin Rafferty would have to get his kicks some other way than by baiting her to the point of screaming.

"Do you know what they call this kind of weather in Ireland?" Devlin asked.

Keeping in mind her vow to be disgustingly agreeable, she glanced out, catching a glimpse of an old stone church and farther on, soaked haystacks in a field. "Let me think," she murmured, tapping a thoughtful finger against her cheek to support the fraud that she had a mad desire to discuss the weather with him. "What would they call a rainy day in Ireland?" Turning to face his square-cut profile, she smiled. The expression hurt, considering her mental state. "This is just a stab in the dark, mind you, but would they perhaps refer to it as—raining?"

The beginnings of a smile tipped the corners of his mouth. "They call it a soft day, when rain falls like this, in a soft, gray curtain."

She smiled again with effort. "That's simply the most charming story I've ever heard."

He cast a glance her way. "Really?" His tone was doubtful. "If that's so charming, then what would you think the Irish call the rain the way it was coming down this morning?"

She had a compulsion to say, *That would be one of Dante's nine stages of hell, wouldn't it?* But she controlled herself. "I'd be simply enchanted beyond words to know," she cooed as vivaciously she could and not die of saccharin overdose.

He frowned, but kept his eye on the curving road, for the pavement was so slick, keeping from skidding off the road required his full attention. "Very funny," he said. "When the wind blows the rain, it's called a desperate day."

"That's so interesting I may faint," she muttered, turning away.

"What's with you, all of a sudden?" he demanded. "You sound like your body's been invaded by a singles-bar airhead."

She smiled like the agreeable idiot she was trying to portray, remembering her vow to ward off any arguments. "That's fascinating. Aren't you the clever one?" Then, with a pleasant expression that was difficult to maintain, she turned away.

The only sound in the car for a long time was the radio, where a woman with a voice like a throaty Joan Baez was singing in Gaelic. The mellow songs would have been pleasing and restful, had Laura's mood been less distraught.

After half an hour, she could no longer fight her urge to turn and check his expression. She could tell by his tone, when he'd last spoken, that he wasn't as happy as he'd been when the ride began. Well, that was fine! It appeared her ploy to upset his contented little argumentative applecart was working. How odd that she wasn't more comfortable with her handiwork. She was forced to admit to herself, now, that the strained quiet between them was infinitely more nerve-racking than any argument would have been.

"Are you hungry?" he asked, making her nearly jump through the roof at his unexpected question.

"I'm fine," she fibbed, not looking his way.

"The *hell* you are," he boomed, shocking her so with his angry tone that she jerked around to face him. His jaw was clenched, his eyes narrowed in a deep frown. "Your stomach's roaring like a lion. What's the reason for this stupid I'm-going-to-be-irritatingly-obliging attitude all of a sudden?"

She spread her hands over her stomach in a fruitless effort to stifle her hunger pangs. She'd had no idea the little noises had been audible over the radio music. Embarrassment flamed her cheeks, but before she could devise an excuse, he said gruffly, "Not far ahead, there used to be a public house that served good salmon sandwiches on homemade brown bread. If it's still there, I'll stop and get you one."

"I don't want to waste any more time than necessary," she muttered.

"Your boss wouldn't consider taking a few minutes off to eat a meal here and there as wasting time. Most people eat, Laura, even on business trips abroad."

"I know that," she retorted more sharply than she'd meant to. She stirred uneasily, not wanting to think about the fact that her problem didn't stem from the idea that *eating* would be a waste of precious time, but from the fear of lingering with Devlin at an intimate little table in some fire-lit pub, loitering over a steamy cup of Irish coffee.

She was afraid to look into those troubled blue eyes. That steady, earnest regard was hard to ignore. It awakened some deeply-buried part of her, some lonely corner of her being that longed for the gentle touch of another human.

Ever since she'd first seen Devlin, Laura had been afraid of whatever it was about him that drew her, afraid of the tug she felt, afraid that she would not be able to escape it forever. She kept reminding herself that she had her daughter to consider. Unfortunately, her body was ignoring her brain's command to shun this man and his damned, seductive eyes.

Laura prayed that this *second* Kathleen would put an end to her search for the missing Kincade heir, and that by tomorrow at this time, she would be on a plane back to Florida, winging away from Devlin Rafferty and whatever it was that was short-circuiting her good sense.

In the pub, she gulped down her salmon sandwich, then vaulted for the door, leaving Devlin scrambling to pay the ruddy proprietor.

Without more than a word or two, they took the car ferry across the Shannon estuary into County Clare, a land of fertile farms scattered across rolling hills, wedded closely to the expanse of the River Shannon.

Laura managed to doze fitfully as the afternoon wore on, but she got no real rest. Her dreams were overrun by menacing, shimmering blue whirlpools, sucking her in, drowning her. She struggled to surface, to fight the downward pull. Terrified, and with a sense of doom, she woke with a start and an audible gasp. When she furtively looked Devlin's way to check if he'd noticed, she was mortified by the concern on his face. There could be no doubt that he was aware that her dreams had been disturbed. But, to her relief, he asked no questions.

THEY HEADED THROUGH Ennis, with its narrow, winding streets, and on westward through "burren country," as Devlin called it, a barren stretch of land with an eerie, lunar-like terrain and an enchanting array of rare flowers.

A little farther on, to her surprise, Devlin stopped the car along some cliffs that overlooked the ocean, and shifted to look at her. "Would you like to get out and stretch? The Cliffs of Moher have a spectacular view."

The Atlantic lay before them, extending off into a hazy infinity. The sun had broken through heavy clouds momentarily, giving the ocean swells a perilous, glittery beauty—reminding Laura of a certain man's uneasy blue eyes.

"Come on," she heard, as a hand came down and encircled her wrist, tugging her from her side of the car. She hadn't even noticed that he'd gotten out and come around to open her door.

Somehow powerless to object, she allowed herself to be led to the edge of the high cliff, where far below, waves were pounding the craggy, vertical wall of rock.

"How high are we?" she asked in a thin little voice, giving away her fear of heights.

"About seven hundred feet above sea level," he said, as she cautiously peeked over the edge to glimpse the long, horrifying drop to the sea.

"I love it here," he went on. "The air is so clean you can almost drink it."

His fondness for this place deeply touched her. Unable to stop herself, she asked, "What is it you've come here to find, Devlin?"

The light in his eyes went out, and he winced before he turned away. A stiff breeze ruffled his hair as he stared out toward the West and the distant horizon. "I don't know," he said, at last. "Ireland, for me, is a mixture of innocence and wisdom. I suppose I need—" he glanced at her, his eyes full of sadness "—a good dose of both."

He looked back out at the ocean. As he watched the waves thunder against the cliffs, she studied his face— his clenched jaw and narrowed eyes—wondering what tragic drama he was silently reliving. "Devlin?" she ventured at last.

He turned, and she was appalled to glimpse something hard and hateful in his eyes before he could mask it and pass her one of his counterfeit smiles. Still, even for a fake, that smile affected her pulse rate.

"What, Laura?" he asked, sounding surprisingly at ease.

She smiled, too, all at once wanting to be a pleasant companion. This time, her effort wasn't devious or contrived. She only knew that Devlin needed something happy to dwell on right now, and she wanted to help. It was crazy how this man had the power to fling her from one emotional extreme to the other—from raging annoyance to downright tenderness—with a single, unwitting glimpse into his tortured soul.

"How often have you visited Ireland? You seem to know so much about the place," she said, hoping the subject would lighten his mood.

They shared a brief but pleasing smile before he said, "My folks honeymooned at the Dingle Bay Country House. Then, several times after that, our family spent a week at Dingle Bay, then a couple more traveling around Ireland during Dad's summer vacation from school."

He placed his hands into his back jeans pockets. "After Dad died, I brought mother over here a few times. When I was twenty-five, she passed away, and the last ten years, my job—" He frowned, then a small smile found its way back to his lips. "We'd better get going." Taking her arm, he guided her toward the car. "And to keep you from dropping off into those nightmares of yours, I'll tell you the legend of the leprechaun when we get on the road."

Once in the car and traveling along the route that edged the cliffs, she said, "If it's that fiction about leprechauns having a pot of gold, I've heard it. Everybody's heard it. Besides, when I was a kid I saw the movie, *Finian's Rainbow*."

He chuckled. "Shut up and listen, you skeptic."

"Oh, for Pete's sake. I suppose this is the price I must pay for the ride."

"Part of it," he said. Laura glanced his way. His expression was impassive, so she decided the erotic nuance she'd thought she'd heard in his words must have been her imagination.

"Okay," he was continuing, "according to the legend, our leprechaun friend has a pot of gold hidden somewhere, and if caught with it, he has to give it up to whoever finds it."

"*Finian's Rainbow* made that very clear," she informed him with mock severity.

"Didn't I tell you to shut up?" he admonished with a grin.

She rolled her eyes, but made no further comment.

"As I was saying before I was interrupted," he went on, "since our leprechaun was a sly fellow, he could fool people by making them look away for an instant while he escaped into the forest."

"Hurray for him," she cut in, drawing his disapproving glance. "I know. Shut up, Laura," she muttered.

Still grinning, he continued to watch the road. "Anyway, a story is told of a man who forced a leprechaun to take him to the bush where the gold was buried. The man, being clever himself, tied a red handkerchief to the bush in order to recognize the spot again. Then he ran home for a shovel. He was gone only three minutes, but when he returned to dig, there was a red handkerchief on every bush in the forest."

He paused, and Laura gave him a narrowed look. "So, what's the point? When you go for the gold, dig with your hands?"

He smiled at her. It was obvious that Devlin was a happier man when speaking about a land and a people he'd grown to love. "You're very witty," he teased. "Actually, the story just points out the Irish sense of fun."

In the face of his disarming expression, she didn't even have an urge to be sarcastic about his infernal "little people."

"If that story makes you happy, Devlin, then I'm happy, too," she said, meaning it.

He inclined his head, glancing at her with an odd look—somehow triumphant—but said nothing more.

Laura sat in confused silence as they meandered along the coast road, wondering what that look could have meant.

KATHLEEN SMYTHE'S HOME towered before them, a lofty and massive three-story country house built of unpolished marble. Connected to the central manse were colonnades that curved gracefully forward, joining two smaller sections to the main house. One of those appeared to be a stable.

"Good grief," Laura breathed, as their car chugged along the paved, tree-shaded drive. "If this Kathleen did give birth to the heir to the Kincade fortune, that kid's no Irish waif."

"Unless she had to give the baby away secretly years ago."

Laura thought about that as they pulled to a halt before a wide set of stairs that rose higher than the roof of the car. She wondered if a woman who was a widow of obvious means would allow her own child to live less well than she. Laura couldn't imagine such a thing.

A FEW MINUTES LATER, they were back in the car. Mrs. Smythe was still not at home. The butler had told them they could wait, but Devlin had taken it upon himself to decline, saying they would be back in an hour.

"Where are we going?" Laura asked, not at all put out that he'd taken over. She didn't relish the idea of sitting stiffly in some cold, formal chamber twiddling her thumbs, waiting to be granted an audience with the grand Mrs. Kathleen Smythe.

"I thought you might enjoy seeing a bridge," he said, as they left the mansion grounds. "It's not too far on east."

"A bridge?" She eyed him, suspicious. "I could be wrong, but haven't we already seen about a zillion bridges today?"

His chuckle was deep and sexy. "Not like the Bella-corick Bridge."

She was puzzled, but attempted to relax. It surprised her to notice she could now sit in the front seat without cringing in horror as cars zoomed by them on the wrong side. That very probably could be attributed to the fact that by comparison *Devlin* disturbed her so much more.

She started when they pulled to a stop before a picturesque stone bridge. "This is it?" she asked, still puzzled, for it seemed like a thousand others.

He smiled at her, and she noticed a devilish glint in his eyes. "What are you going to do, push me off?"

He merely indicated the bridge with a nod. "Come on. You'll see."

Near the platform's brink, he picked up a stone about the size of a baseball and surprised Laura by thrusting it into her hands. "Here," he said. "Toss it along the railing."

"You want me to throw a rock at the bridge?" she asked, then added sarcastically, "Don't you want me to close my eyes and make a wish first? I mean, I never throw a rock at a bridge back in the States unless I've—"

"Throw the damn rock, Laura," he commanded, his voice gentle. When she peered doubtfully at him, he repeated with a grin. "Throw the rock."

So she tossed the rock into the air. It arced upward, then plummeted down to skid along the wet surface of the northern parapet.

She shot Devlin a shocked look and whispered, "Was that—*music* . . . ?"

He winked at her and nodded.

"But how?" she breathed.

"Follow me," he said, bending to pick up a small boulder. Advancing forward, he put it on the same northern wall of the bridge and slid it along. Just as it had been with Laura's stone, the structure once again miraculously gave off tinkling notes.

Devlin jogged along behind the stone, sliding it again and again. The faster he ran across the bridge, propelling his stone, the more melodious and magical the music became.

Laura was amazed and dashed headlong through puddles, unheedful of the fact that she was soaking her shoes. The elfin symphony bounded with them, as Devlin skidded the stone along, thrilling her heart with the unexpected magic and charm of the place.

Once they'd reached the far side of the bridge, Laura was out of breath and laughing. Devlin was laughing, too. It was the first time she'd heard him really laugh. The rich, exuberant sound of it filled the still countryside with warmth, and was every bit as magical and thrilling as the musical bridge.

"Oh, Devlin . . ." she said. Caught up in the exhilaration of the moment, she threw her arms about his neck. "That was wonderful. How does it work?"

"No one knows," he said, his voice very near. With a start, Laura realized what she'd done, and tried to move away, but his strong arms drew her firmly against him. "Would you like to hear the legend of the bridge?"

His gaze held hers with a tenderness that made it difficult for her to concentrate on what he'd asked. Alarm bells went off in her brain, and she knew she must separate herself from him. Right now. Odd, though, her body wasn't working very hard at that. "Does everything in this country . . . have a legend attached?" She winced at how breathless she sounded. His hands were moving along her spine, bringing a long-banked fire to life inside her. She swallowed, "Devlin, I . . ."

"Shut up, Laura," he ordered huskily, as his mouth covered hers with an urgent hunger. His scorching kiss sent shock waves sizzling through her. Fearing she would lose the strength in her legs and tumble over the side of the bridge, plunging to her death, she clung even more desperately to his broad shoulders.

The taste of his mouth was dangerous, delicious, as his knowing lips explored, nibbled and coaxed, leaving her lips throbbing, her body craving more.

She'd fought against the possibility of this moment from the first instant they'd met, but here she was, snuggled in his powerful embrace, yearning for the intimacy of his body, and gratified by the feel of his erection pressed against her belly.

His lips, hard and searching, seared a path down her neck, and she arched reflexively, gasping and panting, reveling in the touch of his hands doing erotic, stimulating things to her back and the curve of her hip.

He lifted his lips from the pulsing hollow of her throat. With a husky whisper, he said, "Laura, Laura, I knew it would be like this. I knew from the first we were meant to be lovers...."

His startling assertion slapped her back to reality, and she was seized by a suffocating dread. What did she think she was doing, allowing this man such liberties out here in front of God and everyone? She had no intention of letting him take her to bed!

Gathering her strength, she pressed away from him, crying, "Devlin—don't say that. I—I didn't come to Ireland to have an affair with a stranger!"

"Neither did I, Laura," he assured her, his soft-spoken affirmation granting her a ray of hope that he, too, had regained his senses.

But, when he lifted his head, his eyes were filled with desire. His expression held no acknowledgment of her rejection, no hint that he didn't fully intend for them to writhe naked together, very soon, tangled blissfully in clean Irish sheets, tucked away in some quaint village inn.

He flashed a roguish smile that provoked wayward and wanton impulses tingling in her core. She grew flushed and giddy, not wanting to dwell on what his look promised.

With a gentle kiss on the tip of her nose, he repeated softly, "Neither did I...."

Laura swallowed hard, experiencing dread and anticipation. She stared into his handsome, confident face, unable to move or speak. The bold glitter in his eyes was declaring without question that Laura *would* have an affair with a stranger in Ireland—and that that stranger would be Devlin Rafferty.

5

THE BUTLER LED DEVLIN and Laura down a long corridor toward a remote corner of the mansion. As their footsteps echoed loudly on the mauve-and-white Victorian tiles, Laura scanned the dour portraits of Kathleen's ancestors that lined the walls. She grimaced, imagining their harsh eyes boring into her, disapproving of her quest. She shook off her wild fantasies. She was being foolish. After all, she was here to give Kathleen's child—if it *was* Kathleen's child—a substantial fortune. Besides, with her husband gone, how could the truth of a bastard child hurt Kathleen now?

At last they entered a drawing room. Laura took a seat beside Devlin on a leather couch across from a cheery peat fire.

The rest of the chamber was cast in deep shadow. There was just one long, narrow window, and only a limited amount of light streamed through the stained-glass design of blue and yellow birds soaring in a teal sky. The walls were covered in blue sculpted velvet, darkening the room further. On either side of the couch sat a leather chair of the same cushiony design. Beside one of them was a fat world globe; next to the other was a spindly oval table containing a Waterford hurricane lamp, the light of a flickering, lavender-scented candle magnifying the brilliance of the handcrafted Irish crystal. Clustered near the lamp were two elegant Waterford doves and a crystal owl paperweight.

Against two of the room's walls were wide book-shelves six feet tall, with paintings of birds adorning the remainder of the wall to the ceiling. A niche, at about head height on either side of the window, contained striking bronzes of more birds. A long desk, butted against the back of the couch, was cluttered with small porcelain pieces. These, too, were depictions of birds, either on the wing or perched on a porcelain branch.

"Apparently, Kathleen likes birds," Laura asided quietly, startled by the strange echo her words created. They both looked up at the curved ceiling, which was decorated with ornamental plaster.

"That curve must have something to do with the echo in here," Devlin said, his comment echoing back to them. Glancing over at her as the reverberations of his voice ended, he grinned disarmingly.

She felt a thrill at the sight, and averted her gaze. Since his kiss not long ago, she'd been able to think of very little else. The trip back to Kathleen's country house had been strained—at least for her. Devlin, on the other hand, had appeared quite contented. She'd tried several times to reiterate that she had absolutely no intention of having an affair with him, but he'd merely smiled an infuriating smile and said nothing. How could she argue with a man so maddeningly satisfied with himself? Where was his argumentative nature when she needed it?

But now, in this intimate, dusky setting, surrounded by beautiful antiques and nestled before a snug fire, she felt a growing, unrepentant urge to be hauled into his embrace again, to be swept away by his kisses to a place without guilt or repercussions.

"Nice tits," Devlin murmured, shocking Laura out of her wayward reverie as thoroughly as if she'd been doused with ice water.

Appalled by his lewd comment, she gaped at him. "I beg your pardon," she snapped, affronted, her echo every bit as disdainful. "You may have kissed me, Mr. Rafferty, but one kiss doesn't give you any right to be crude!"

There was a twinkle glittering somewhere in those blue depths. Raking her with a slow, teasing regard, he offered, "You're very nice looking, Laura, but . . ." Indicating the leaded-glass window, he explained, "I was talking about the *blue* tits in the stained glass. I gather you're not much into the local bird population."

"Like heck, you are!" she accused.

He merely grinned.

With strained civility, she reminded him, "I'm not much into the local *anything*, if you'll recall. I've only been in Ireland for twenty-four hours." Made squeamish by his steady perusal, she edged farther away.

"I'm sorry, Laura," he said, though his tone was far from repentant; worse, the rich reverberation of his voice seemed to be openly laughing at her.

Unwilling to reply or look his way, she cleared her throat and focused on one of the infernal blue tits suspended forever in a dive toward a glass rose.

The couch they were sharing was five feet long. She'd scooted as far as she could to one end, and, thankfully, Devlin had not crowded her. Still, his nearness was playing havoc with her nerves, for he'd slung an arm across the back cushion, and his long fingers were a scant inch from her shoulder. She chewed on her lower lip, praying that their tardy hostess, Mrs. Kathleen Smythe, would soon appear, and that in the meantime, Laura wouldn't give in to a wayward desire to leap into Devlin's arms right here on Mrs. Smythe's couch.

She shuddered. *Get hold of yourself, Laura!* she berated, clutching her hands in a tense ball in her lap.

"Did you say something?" Devlin asked.

She jumped, shaking her head. "N-n-no . . ." By the time she got through stuttering out her answer, it sounded as though a whole group of stammering idiots had responded in the negative.

He grinned again. "The room's getting pretty crowded," he quipped. "Maybe I should leave."

I'd pay to see that, her mind screamed, but before she could say anything, the paneled door swung wide and a woman hurried inside.

"My dears," she warbled in a crisp English accent. "I do apologize for being so unforgivably tardy. Birding, you know. Our feathered friends have become my very life since Jonathan, my dear departed husband, went to his reward. I don't mind telling you, today was dashing sport. We had a rousing chase after a sparrow hawk. Nearly broke my blasted neck, but . . ." She grinned. "I don't suppose you've come all this way to discuss bird-watching or an old woman's foolishness."

Laura felt an uncomfortable prick. Mrs. Smythe was very close—a bastard child might be considered by some as a *very* foolish thing. But she shook her head, staring at the portly, chattery woman as her equally chattery echo died away. So this was Mrs. Kathleen Smythe? Not at all the grand lady Laura had expected, she was clad in blue jeans rolled up to reveal scuffed and muddied hiking boots and heavy, red woolen socks. She sported a man's black-and-green plaid flannel shirt under an equally masculine brown tweed jacket. Her gray-streaked hair was hidden, except for some fly-away strands, beneath a gentleman's patch tweed cap. She looked more like the English counterpart of a rather natty bag lady than the wealthy mistress of a huge country estate. Her skin was quite ruddy, her smile completely engaging. Penetrating green eyes snapped with wisdom and vitality.

The older woman startled Laura by drawing out a yellowed meerschaum pipe and flopping down on an adjacent leather chair. After tamping in tobacco from a pouch she'd pulled from her jacket pocket, she lit up. Without comment, she puffed deeply for a long moment until the tobacco glowed red.

Her eyes closed, Kathleen breathed a sigh of contentment before seeming to notice her visitors again. As soon as she did, she frowned. "What! No tea? Bloody fool! I told McCann to bring us a pot!" She bounced up, before Laura could protest, and went to yank irritably on a long tapestry ribbon with a royal blue tassel that bobbed wildly under her determined fist. After jerking several times, she returned and plopped back down, draping a plump leg over one arm of her chair. "There, now. That ought to bring him on the run. That was my secret code for, 'Get the bloody pot of tea up here, you idiot!'" She grinned again. Laura noticed she had a fleshy mouth and a rather prominent gap between her two front teeth—an engaging gap that seemed to suit her.

"So . . ." She considered Laura's face more seriously, and then Devlin's, before going on, "I understand you wanted to see me about something concerning Dingle Bay Country House." With her teeth clenched on her pipe stem, she said, "That was long ago—a dear time with fond memories—but another life for me." Pausing, she took a deep puff. "I do love a mystery, so please begin," she coaxed, through a smoke-filled exhale.

After seeing this candid woman in action, Laura didn't see much need for delicacy, but one never knew. She began cautiously, anyway, "Mrs. Smythe, we're here—"

"*Kathleen*, dear girl," the older woman insisted, sucking on her pipe. "Please, do call me Kathleen. As you may have noticed, I am not a woman of pretension."

Laura nodded. "Thank you." She couldn't help but dart a quick glance at Devlin. He was sitting quietly, watching her with eyes that were both amused and curious. Apparently he wanted to see how she handled the situation. Well, she appreciated his silence, at least. Shifting her scrutiny back to Kathleen, she began again, "Kathleen, do you recall . . ."

Her sentence faded away when the butler entered with a silver tea service on a heavy silver tray. Kathleen wrenched around and glared at him. "There you are, you brainless dolt! Bring that here immediately. My throat is simply parched!"

The butler was a rather handsome, silver-haired gentleman of about Kathleen's age. His mild response to her harangue was the composed lift of one silver brow and a rather bored, "Your wish is my command, your highness."

Laura couldn't miss the sarcasm of his words and was completely baffled by the repartee.

McCann crossed to the low table in front of the couch and positioned the tray in its center. Laura noticed that besides the tea and cups, there was a silver bowl with a white linen cloth covering something that smelled wonderful.

When he straightened, the servant intoned, "The potato rolls were not quite done until this minute, my queen. Shall I take myself up to the roof and fling myself to my death for my tardiness?"

Laura frowned. She glanced from the deadpan face of the butler to Mrs. Smythe, who was grinning and puffing. "I think not, this time, McCann. Take yourself to your quarters. I shall dole out your punishment later."

"Shall I chain myself to the bedpost, m'lady?"

She waved her pipe as if to say she didn't really care. "I shall leave to your judgment the degree of your punishment."

He bowed slightly. "Thank you, my most gracious sovereign. I grovel at your royal feet for sparing my worthless life yet again. I shall await you...in chains." With that, he silently left.

When he'd closed the door behind him, Kathleen burst into gravelly guffaws that bounced around the chamber like rifle blasts. "McCann is quite the wag. He was once the master of this estate, but the poor chap fell upon hard times. When I purchased the place, I kept him around. I'll grant, I don't keep him about merely for his drollery or out of pity. I, shall we say, knew from the first moment we met that I could put that talented tongue to much more delightful uses. And not to boast, but I was right. McCann has proven to be quite an exquisite lover."

Laura's mouth dropped open, and when Kathleen noticed, she grinned that gap-toothed grin, and a stream of smoke slithered out from between her front teeth. "My dear child, even a widow of my years has ... *needs*." With a knowing nod, she added almost dreamily, "Oh, my, yes, when one says 'The butler did

it' within these walls, they are speaking of a wicked-
ness abundantly more gratifying than has ever been
depicted in those uninspired mystery novels."

"Would anyone like some tea?" Devlin asked, lifting
the pot. Laura noted that his hands were big and steady,
as though he weren't even slightly shocked. She supposed, as a lawyer, he'd heard it all.

"By all means, my boy," Kathleen trilled. "Three
sugars and a large measure of cream, if you please."

Once they were all sipping the strong black tea from
delicate Belleek cups, Laura began again, "Kathleen,
do you recall ever meeting a man by the name of Joshua
Kincade when you worked at the Dingle Bay Country
House?"

Kathleen paused in the midst of a sip. Laura couldn't
tell if she was in deep thought or in pain.

After a momentary pause, the woman finished her
sip. "It seems the name is familiar...."

Laura helped. "He was an American film director
spending about six months there while making a
movie."

Kathleen sipped again, then looked up. "Ah. The
devilish handsome young blood from America. The
filmmaker? Kincade, you say? Yes." She put down her
cup and picked up the bowl of potato rolls, offering
them around. "He was still there when I vacated my
post and went to England."

"Yes," Laura coaxed. "We're looking for a...relative
of his. A child." When she saw Kathleen's brows dip in
the midst of lathering butter across her roll, she hurried on, "Actually, this individual wouldn't be a child
any longer. He—or she—would be around thirty-five
years old, today."

The portly woman examined Laura's serious face. "What are you saying, my dear? That that unprincipled scapegrace spilled his seed here in Ireland, and now he's looking for the unfortunate mother and child?"

Laura was amazed by the woman's perceptiveness, but she supposed anyone who was having a fling with her butler would be able to quickly grasp the fact that others, too, could be involved in unorthodox sexual antics. "Exactly." she said. Now came the hard part. Clearing her throat, Laura began, "The only information we have as to the identity of the woman who was . . . involved with Josh Kincade, is the name Kathleen. . . . " She allowed the explanation to die away so the weight of her suggestion could penetrate.

The widow's eyes widened, and she stopped chewing on her roll. "Kathleen, you say?" she asked, after swallowing the bit of food. "And you think that Kathleen might be myself?"

Laura smiled weakly, but encouragingly. "Mr. Kincade retired to Florida and had become reclusive in his later years. In a notarized letter that was found among his things, he stated he wanted to do right by his child and willed his entire fortune to him—or her. The bequest was discovered when representatives of the Treasury Department were called in to handle the disbursement of his property. Since he had neither relatives nor legal counsel at the time of his death, the State has the responsibility of locating his heir. I'm here representing the State in that regard."

Kathleen looked from one to the other. "Heir? So you're saying this Kincade is dead, and that this child is going to come into money, then?"

"A small inheritance," Laura hedged.

Kathleen laughed, and the sharp, gritty sound bounced around them. "Don't fret, my dear. It is of no concern to me how large the legacy is, for I am filthy rich, as you surely see. To be frank, I cannot be the handsome scamp's forsaken Kathleen. The truth be told, when I was a child of twelve, I had a hemorrhage, and the surgeon had to remove the workings for bearing children. That is the very reason I became a nanny, to be around the precious tykes I could not bear. Then I met Jonathan, and the love didn't mind that I could not have children. The dear man—he always said we needed nothing more than each other. Ours was a wild, passionate love." She shook her head sadly. "No, my dear, I am not the Kathleen you are searching for." This time when she offered the rolls around, Laura took one. As she split it open and spread butter on it, Kathleen surprised her with, "If my mind is right on this, I would say Kathleen is not even the name of the poor woman you seek."

"Why do you say that?" Devlin asked.

"It is just that I do recall some talk around that time about one of the housemaids. A sweet, shy, lovely child who took Mr. Kincade his high tea each afternoon, and seemed to linger in his chamber—" She cut herself off. *"That's it!"* she cried, banging the table with a fistful of roll, making the silver and china clatter. "That's it, of course. Kathleen was not the name of the woman, but the chamber. The Kathleen Chamber! His room. That American, Josh Kincade, stayed that entire time in Ireland in the *Kathleen* Chamber. Back in those days the Dingle Bay Country House called rooms by genteel old Irish names such as Kathleen." She shook her head. "Poor Maureen. That was it. I recall now. Maureen . . . Maureen Renny. The girl was truly smitten by the American." Tisk-tisking, she went on, "So, that shy thing succumbed to his wooing and was left, disgraced and alone, and this Kincade fellow, after so much time, couldn't even recall her right name."

"Maureen Renny?" Laura repeated, rummaging in her bag for her notebook. "Are you sure? Do you know what happened to this girl?"

"Well," Kathleen said, taking a sip of her tea. "I did hear that she's been gone from Dingle for a while. The story was, she went visiting kin but I don't know where. Last I heard she was given employment at an orphanage in Galway. I married my Jonathan about then and lost contact with my friends at Dingle Bay. I fear I know nothing beyond that. I'd wager it's poor Maureen you should be looking for, my dear. And if Maureen Renny did bear a child by this Kincade, I hope the fortune eases her life in some way."

"At least she'd be assured her child will live well from now on," Laura said hopefully, knowing that no amount of money would ever make up for the hurt of rejection, the disillusionment and the utter shame of bearing an illegitimate child in a country of strict, traditional morals.

Taking up her pipe again, Kathleen puffed thoughtfully. Laura knew the widow was thinking the same sad thought. After a moment, Kathleen murmured, "Godspeed to you, then—for both their sakes."

GALWAY, FAMOUS FOR ITS seafood and sunsets, was a bustling city of winding streets and ancient, romantic lanes lined with shops and pubs. It had grown dark when they reached the city and was too late to visit the Galway Foundling Home. Instead, they settled on a pub that had rooms for rent upstairs, and booked two for the night. That done, Laura and Devlin returned to the pub for dinner.

"I can't believe we came right through here this afternoon on our way to Bangor," Laura sighed as she picked at her prawns.

"I'd think you'd be used to this sort of thing in your work—leads that take you back and forth over the same territory," Devlin said.

"I suppose. I guess it just seems more frustrating when you're—"

"With somebody who makes you uncomfortable?" Devlin interrupted softly.

Her gaze shot to his face. How perceptive of him, she thought darkly. Yes. That was certainly part of it. She'd hoped their association would be over by now. Ever since the kiss on the bridge this afternoon, she'd been a mess. "No . . . of course not," she lied. "I—I was going to say . . . in a foreign country."

He grinned that knowing grin but there was no glimmer of amusement in his eyes. "What is it, Laura, that makes you so afraid of commitment?"

She winced. "Commitment!" she charged helplessly, leaning closer. "*What* commitment? You were talking about a tumble in the sheets."

He shook his head. "No, I wasn't, Laura, and I think you know that. I think you know how I feel about you. You knew it yesterday in your loft, when I asked you if you believed in—"

"And *you* remember what I said," she retorted, refusing to allow him to say the word. "To be honest," she said, "I have been committed in my day. And if I even thought about doing it again—especially after one day's acquaintance—I'd be nuts enough to *have* to be committed! Do I make myself clear?"

His mouth twisting wryly, he said, "You're cute when you're irrational."

She stiffened. "Don't patronize me. I don't have affairs with someone I've only known one day, and I certainly don't *commit* myself to them!"

"One and a half," he pointed out before taking a bite.

"*What?*" she demanded, flustered and upset.

When he was again looking at her, he said, "We've known each other one-and-a-half days."

"Oh! That makes all the difference, then," she blurted. "Usually, after knowing a man for one-and-a-half days, I throw off all my clothes and play catch-me games in the first handy park! We cause a few random heart attacks, but that can't be helped. Sexual fulfillment is my life."

"Are you finished?" he asked, his voice tense.

"If you mean with dinner, I think I'll have dessert."

"I don't give a damn about dessert," he growled.

"That's your privilege, but I'm having a meringue filled with chocolate mousse."

"On a soft day in Ireland, meringues get chewy. You may be disappointed," he cautioned, clearly struggling to maintain his calm.

"Mind your own business, Mr. Rafferty," she flared. "What I choose to eat or not to eat—er—" An off-color vision skidded across her mind. Swallowing, she rushed on, "Anyway, it's none of your business!"

"*I'm making it my business,*" he stated grimly, vaulting to stand. "Dammit, I love you, Laura. I've been in love with you from the first moment I saw you. You know it, and someday you're going to tell me why that frightens you. Chew on *that,* why don't you." Before she could gather her wits, he'd stomped out of the pub and into the gentle rain of the Irish night.

When the shock of his revelation wore off, Laura noticed the room had gone deathly quiet. She glanced around and was dismayed to see all eyes were on her. Good Lord! Apparently Devlin's declaration had been loud enough for everyone in the pub to hear. She felt herself color as someone began to applaud. Pretty soon, the room was filled with laughter and clapping. It was obvious that an affirmation of love, no matter how angrily spoken, was worthy of a standing ovation, even in her embarrassing circumstance. It was possible, of course, they were all stumbling, staggering drunk, and would have clapped if a rat had slithered across a table. Or maybe, this was just another insidious example of the Irish sense of "fun."

Well, *she'd* had better times getting her teeth drilled! Humiliated, she pushed out of the booth and hurried from the crowded tavern toward the staircase that led to the rooms, ignoring as best she could the well-wishing pats and hearty squeezes of callused hands on hers while she made her escape. As she mounted the stairs, tears welled in her eyes. How could Devlin have done that to her in such a public place?

She prayed—harder than she'd ever prayed in her life—that tomorrow she would see Galway in the rearview mirror of an Irish *bus*, as she headed out of Maureen Renny's newly enriched life—and Devlin Rafferty's deluded one.

6

HEEDLESS OF THE RAIN, Devlin roamed along the docks. At the most emotionally destitute point in his life, he'd found the woman that was meant for him. And she wanted him like she wanted a train wreck. Cursing, he jammed his hands into his jeans pockets and accelerated his pace. The cobbled lane where he paced was lit by the dim glow of street lamps.

He heard a sharp cry in the distance, and stood stock-still, listening for the next sound—expecting a shriek of terror. But almost immediately there was a giggle, followed by the deep laugh of a man. It was a couple. Obviously lovers. He could see them now, illuminated by the beam of a lamp as they dashed arm in arm from a secluded doorway to a waiting car. The woman squealed again. Clearly, her previous high-pitched cry had only been part of this couple's noisy brand of foreplay.

He exhaled heavily, lifting his face to the rain. He allowed the cool water to sluice over him as he struggled to regain his composure. But that brief female cry had brought it all back. That night not so long ago when his friend, Tony DeMotto of the homicide squad, had called him and growled, "Come on over, Counselor. See what your genius has caused. I hope it makes you good and sick." Tony had sounded like a bitter, weary old man that night.

Devlin had gone. And what he'd seen still made him sick. For the millionth time, he recalled her vividly. Sixteen years old and . . .

He ran both hands roughly over his face in a desperate attempt to wipe away the gruesome image. It had been raining just like this, but *that* setting had been far from picturesque—a garbage-littered back alley in a Chicago low-rent district.

Her sweet, babyish face loomed in his mind. Bile rose up to choke him as he pictured, once again, the ugly specter of what one human being could do to another. His knees buckled and he pitched forward, overwhelmed by gut-wrenching pain as the memory he'd been trying to block from his consciousness rolled back with the force of an out-of-control bulldozer.

His breath coming in heavy, audible gasps, he veered toward a wall, lunging hard against the stone surface. He pressed his face to the cold, wet stone. Devlin was too lost in his anguish and self-hatred to care about the muffled, wounded howls that issued up from his throat. He didn't care who saw him—he didn't deserve any man's compassion; nor did he want pity.

This was his hell—a well-deserved hell on earth. He'd been blindly arrogant. And because of it, a young girl was dead. Nothing he could do in this world would ever change that. No amount of self-flagellation, no extent of running away, no degree of justification, would make things right again. He'd been told to go on with his life. But the girl's innocent face kept coming back, haunting him, damning him to the lowest reaches of hell. He was a man cursed, alone, without hope.

Suddenly there had been Laura—his ray of hope in the black, bottomless pit. The exquisite irony was, she wanted *nothing* to do with him.

He heard a bitter laugh, and realized with some shock that it had come from him. Yes, it was worth a laugh. Maybe the fates had meant him to find Laura, and to know she was the only woman in the world for him. Maybe his ultimate punishment would be that she could *never* be his.

With another low chuckle, he muttered, "*Mea culpa*, Tony. You were right. The genius was dead wrong. . . ."

LAURA FELT A LITTLE better at breakfast. At least it was sunny this morning. What really had lightened her heart was the fact that she'd called her daughter last night at her mother's house, and her five-year-old had sounded fine. It had been hard to try to explain, again, where she was, and why, but Sally had seemed contented that "Mama" would eventually return. Laura was grateful for that, at least.

She didn't like overrelying on her mother to baby-sit. A child like Sally could be a bit of a problem, at times. And, though Emma loved her grandchild, she was a high-strung woman, and the pitying looks and whispers she got when she was out in public with Sally invariably upset her. Besides, Emma periodically suffered from arthritis, so there were times when Emma found lifting Sally painfully difficult. Last night, however, they'd both sounded happy and fine. Laura breathed a sigh of relief, then squelched it when she saw Devlin approaching her corner table.

He seemed taller and somehow remote this morning. Unfortunately that didn't keep her pulse from jumping into high gear when he stood close to her, clad in a rumpled linen shirt with the sleeves rolled up just past his elbows. The shirt was oversize and slouchy, yet managed to appear elegant on his broad frame. The man affected her the same way. He was in pain, yet somehow princely—like a knight-errant fallen from grace.

Devlin continued to stand there silently, his weight shifted onto one leg, his hands thrust deep in his pockets, giving him a careless, sexy air. But his blue eyes, direct and solemn, struck her once again with their tragic beauty. At a loss for words, she continued eating her breakfast.

Without so much as a smile or a good-morning, he asked, "Are you ready to go?"

She managed to swallow her bite of dark bread. "Aren't you going to eat first?"

"I ate some time ago. I've been walking."

She took a last sip of coffee and stood, replacing her napkin on the table. "Where's your jacket?"

"It got wet," he said without inflection as he allowed her to precede him out of the pub to the car. Laura was surprised, considering his aloof, almost-angry manner, that he opened her door for her.

Once he was settled in the driver's seat, she began to unfold her city map. "I think if we go straight ahead for a mile and then turn—"

"I know where it is," he cut in, switching on the engine. "I found it this morning."

"On your walk?"

He pulled out into traffic. "On my walk," he repeated, his sharp-edged profile registering nothing—or at least, nothing pleasant. So she leaned stiffly back, feeling uneasy, which wasn't new for her.

The Galway Foundling Home was a nondescript gray building on a nondescript street. The place was old, but scrubbed and clean. The indoor furnishings were mismatched, but rather than making the place appear makeshift, they gave the home an eclectic charm.

Laura could hear children laughing and chattering in the play yard.

The headmistress's office was small, but lace curtains brightened the window, and a red velvet Victorian couch dominated the space in front of the scarred desk. Old metal file cabinets lined the walls, and numerous photos of beaming children adorned the faded floral wallpaper—children who had been successfully placed in homes, Laura assumed.

The headmistress, Mrs. Margaret O'Sullivan, was in her late forties and had the pinched face and tightly drawn bun of perennial spinster. Her smile, however, brightened her features to reveal the real woman—a warm, generous and openhearted lover of humankind.

When Laura explained her mission, Mrs. O'Sullivan sadly informed them of Maureen Renny's death seven years before. Kind, solitary, shy Maureen Renny had given herself completely to the unwanted children of Ireland, and she was sorely missed. Though she'd earned two weeks' vacation time every year, she'd left the home only rarely. Where Maureen went or what she did on her infrequent holidays remained a mystery to Mrs. O'Sullivan. Maureen had never spoken of them.

"Did she have a child of her own?" Laura asked.

With a firm shake of her head, Mrs. O'Sullivan stated, "Mercy me. Never to me knowledge. The poor soul lived a lonely life and gave her love to the wee ones here. You are indeed welcome to search through the attic. If I recall right, there were a few parcels that were never claimed by kin—if there be kin."

THE NEXT TWO DAYS WERE a grimy, strained eternity for Laura. She and Devlin searched the attic endlessly for the few boxes marked Maureen Renny, then settled down to search through her meager belongings by the faint light of a naked bulb dangling from the ceiling.

"I like Maureen," Laura mused aloud on the evening of the second day. "She cared about her things." Holding up a blouse, yellowed with age, she showed him a small patch, the stitches so tiny and neat it would almost take a magnifying glass to spot the tear. "I wish we could have helped her, too."

"So you think she's the right one?" Devlin asked from where he sat a few feet away. His response startled Laura. He'd spoken so little in the last two days, she'd almost forgotten how deep-pitched his voice was, and the cramped attic seemed to magnify its mellow resonance even more.

"I— Well, yes. I can't explain it. I just have this feeling." She was embarrassed to be so vague, but couldn't really explain. Faced with his skeptical response, she defended, "Haven't you ever had a feeling about something—been *sure* about something you couldn't explain?"

"Once. Yes," he said, his tone tinged with reproach. "I met a young woman in a customs line, who—"

She burst into a fit of loud coughing—not so much because of the dust in the room but to keep him from going on about the dratted love-at-first sight silliness that he kept insisting on bombarding her with in every glance, every nuance of conversation. When would she learn not to present him with opportunities to do so? With dispatch, she began replacing Maureen's clothes into the box.

Still, her thoughts kept returning to the subject. Last night had been the *worst* as far as his unsubtle suggestions went. She'd been forced to sit and squirm through dinner at Mrs. O'Sullivan's apartment, while Devlin had enthralled the woman and her jolly husband, Paddy, with stories about his so-called perfect family. How his father and mother had met and fallen in love at first sight and how he knew he would find his true love that way, too. Margaret and Paddy hadn't helped things by admitting they'd fallen in love when they'd first laid eyes on each other twenty-five years ago at the annual Puck's Fair in her hometown of Killorglin.

As Laura tensely sat there, the three of them had agreed that none other than the kind and loving leprechauns, or *síoga*, had been responsible for the quarter century of wedded bliss Margaret and Paddy had shared. Devlin's gaze, when it shifted in the direction of Laura, had been a disturbing mixture of annoyance and mockery. Though his ploy had irritated her beyond words, she'd found it impossible to turn away from his pointed, sparking stare.

As soon as she could get a word in edgewise, she'd made her excuses about an early morning, and had given Devlin the cold shoulder. Until just now, her speculations about Maureen had made her forget how put out she was with Devlin.

Well, she wasn't going to let his browbeating go on. She'd put an end to their silent battle this minute. "Look, Devlin," she said, getting up and wiping dust from her jeans. "You have every right to believe in this so-called perfect family and this so-called *love at first sight* if the crazy notion pleases you. But leave me out of it!" She swung around and thunked the box back into its original resting place. "I'm in Ireland on business, and you're here on vacation. Period. No leprechauns are involved in our meeting or our future! For your information, if that golden surface on any seemingly perfect family has cause to get scratched, don't be shocked if you find rot underneath!"

As she stalked away from him, he caught her wrist, drawing her into the circle of his arms. "Laura, I'm sorry for whatever's hurt you in your past, but you're wrong," he objected, near her ear. "What my family had proves you're wrong."

His touch was firm and persuasive as his breath teased the hair at her temple. The intimate, thrilling jolt of his groin against her belly made her tingly all over, and she experienced a wild, almost unbearable need to be stroked, to be blessedly naked beneath Devlin.

Horrified at how quickly she weakened around this man, she mustered whatever strength was left in her and reaffirmed her vow to keep her promise to herself and to Sally. "No—*no!* I won't, I can't— Not again..." she gasped, shoving out of his arms, fighting her attraction to him.

She jerked her wrist from his hold and spun away, only to be brought up short when her sneakered foot slammed down inside an old coal bucket. She took another few clanking steps before she could regain her balance.

Then she attempted to shake the bucket loose. Lifting the captured foot, she shook it recklessly, almost losing her balance again. Looking around for a place to perch, she plopped down on an old three-legged stool and shoved.

"Need any help?"

"*No,*" she insisted with a grunt as she pushed to no avail. "And don't you—" she shoved again "—*dare* say anything about me kicking the bucket!"

"I wouldn't joke at a time like this," he assured her, his tone less severe as he came over and squatted to help her.

He managed to pull her foot free, but her shoe was still wedged in the bucket. "Oh, fine!" she observed, with a frustrated sigh.

He finally wrenched the sneaker loose and handed it to her. "No harm done," he said, and Laura cringed at the tone of sympathy in his voice. She didn't want sympathy from this man. She didn't want *any* emotion from him whatsoever.

Fumbling with the laces, she got her shoe on as quickly as she could, muttering, "I didn't see that darned thing there before! No doubt your precious little Sasquatch did this!"

"Why would you say that?" he demanded, standing to tower over her.

"Why shouldn't I beat you to it, for once? What makes this time so different?" she countered.

"For one thing, Sasquatch is the name for Big Foot."

Heat rushed to her cheeks. Yanking the laces tight, she tied them hurriedly. "Very funny. You're a laugh a minute," she gritted. "You know what I meant!"

When the shoe was tied, she took off, descending the stairs from the attic two at a time, but before she was out of earshot, she heard him taunt, "Just for the record, Laura. Who brought up leprechauns, this time?"

It was nearly five o'clock. Dashing first into the little bathroom next to Mrs. O'Sullivan's office, Laura threw water on her face, more to cool her fiery cheeks than to clean off the dust. When she had dried off and taken a few deep breaths, she went out into the hall to be met by Devlin, who was lounging there, his arms crossed over his chest. "Mrs. O'Sullivan's on the phone, but she wants us to wait," he said, his expression less troubled than she'd thought it might be, considering how she'd reacted to their recent quarrel.

Scowling, she leaned against the opposite wall; but that didn't put them far enough apart for her needs at the moment. She still felt an odd ache that had nothing to do with the fact that she'd missed lunch.

"Oh, grand," Mrs. O'Sullivan said with a smile, as she appeared outside her office. "Sure and I was wantin' ta catch ye before ye leave." She held out a piece of paper and handed it to Devlin, which irked Laura no end. But she made no comment about exactly *who* was in charge here, as Mrs. O'Sullivan went on, "I had a thought. So, I went and searched through me old files for the phone number of one of our workers, retired these two years. I found the number and rang her up. And she says to me, she says, Maureen Renny once spoke kindly of a sister, a Myrtle, in Killannin. But, alas, she couldn't recall the surname."

"Myrtle in Killannin," Laura murmured, feeling despondent. "How many might there be?"

"'Tis not much of a town," Mrs. O'Sullivan said. "And 'tis but a wee drive west."

Laura manufactured a smile and put out a hand to the woman. "Well, thank you, Mrs. O'Sullivan. If you can think of anything else, you can contact me through Dingle Bay Country House. I'm still registered there and I check for messages every day."

"That, I'll do," the woman said, shaking Laura's hand. "Now be off with ye, and may the luck o' the leprechauns ride yer shoulder."

Laura managed to retain her smile as she exited the building, but as Devlin was about to get into the car, she halted him, stating, "I think it's time we parted company."

With the car door ajar, he looked at her as though he wasn't sure what she'd said, or possibly, he wasn't sure she was right in the head. "Would you repeat that?" he asked.

She lifted a determined chin. "I said, I think it's best if we part company here. I didn't think this was going to turn into a big deal. And with this Myrtle no-last-name thing, I just don't think it's fair to keep dragging you around."

"Has it occurred to you that I'd let you know if I'd had enough?"

She'd anticipated this argument so she managed not to flinch under his steady regard. "Well . . . it's not that I'm ungrateful, but I think I'd better just take the bus from here on—"

"To Killannin?" he queried, sounding almost amused.

Her stomach knotted with unease. "Why, yes. What's wrong with that? Don't they have roads to Killannin?"

"They have roads."

"Well, then?" she demanded, renewing her intention to leave him *now*, and get on with her life.

"They have roads, Laura," he commented quietly. "But bus service is pretty sparse west of here."

"But I thought you said—"

"Along the west coast, the villages are small and scattered, and the people are pretty independent. It's not like getting from Tallahassee to Orlando."

Darn! Why hadn't she had the guts to rent her own car in the first place? It was her stupid cowardice that was to blame. If she hadn't been such a ninny, she'd be on the road, doing her job, not standing here arguing with a painfully tempting man, wasting precious government bucks!

Deflated, but still determined to be on her own as quickly as she could, she said, "Mind if I drive? I think I could use the practice."

The only evidence that he was surprised was the widening of his eyes. He stepped away from the car and motioned for her to get in. "Shall I alert the media?" he teased, handing her the car keys. "This might be interesting."

She slipped in, managing not to brush against him in the process. "Just watch the map so we don't get lost," she retorted. "I can handle this. I've learned a lot in a few days."

Once behind the wheel—which had the stick shift on the *wrong* side—she squeezed her eyes shut as a feeling of incompetence engulfed her. While Devlin rounded the car, she issued up a quick, desperate prayer that her pride would not force her to kill herself or anyone else with this car. She'd sat next to Devlin watching him drive hour after hour. Hadn't she finally begun to adapt to it? Surely she could do this. Millions of people drove this way, didn't they? Many of them were American tourists. She had to be as smart as—as most of them, didn't she?

Devlin settled himself on the passenger's side and fastened his seat belt before he coaxed, "You might try putting the keys in the ignition first. It helps."

She flashed him a disapproving look. "I'm doing it. I'm doing it."

Once the engine was chugging, she concentrated on the stick shift. When Devlin started to say something, she shushed him, assuring, "Don't be afraid. I have this thing under control."

With a surge of self-confidence, she pulled out into traffic, much relieved to find herself on the correct side of the road, and not involved in a messy head-on collision.

When she tried the stick, the car jerked and the gears made sickly grinding noises, but she finally got them moving along smoothly. Before she knew it, they were headed out of Galway and along the coast, with its deep, curling bays.

"This isn't so hard," she bragged with a grin.

They left the coast road and turned inland. Laura had been driving for thirty minutes or so, and felt quite the professional, when Devlin cleared his throat. "Left right here," he murmured, as though he was afraid if he spoke too loudly he'd spook her.

"What? I turn right here?" she asked, quickly glancing his way.

"No. Left—here, Laura. *Left*, right now." He gestured as the turn loomed.

She swallowed, suddenly flustered. "*Right* here?" she squeaked.

"Yes. But *left!* Hell. Forget it, you can't make it—"

"Oh, left! Right," she gritted determinedly, swerving around the bend on two wheels. The lane was narrow and rutted but she managed to get them straightened out, and grinned with pride.

"Now that you've mastered the left turn, you might try to miss that hay cart," Devlin cautioned, sounding tense.

"What—" Then she saw it, realizing that in her anxiousness, she'd reverted to the old American rule that when you turn left, you cross the lanes to end up on the right. Unfortunately for her, a creaky, donkey-drawn wagon, top-heavy with hay, was headed toward her. Though the old man was slapping his reins, trying to move the animal, it had come to a confused halt in her direct path.

"Go left, Laura, *left!*"

"Oh—Lord!" She was drawing a blank.

"Damn," she heard Devlin mutter when she finally swung the wheel. After whizzing by the terrified elderly gentleman in the cart, Laura found herself being jarred unmercifully as they jounced into an open field, then slammed to an abrupt halt in soft earth.

Dazed, Laura shook her head.

"Are you all right?" came Devlin's concerned reply, as he touched her shoulder.

"Yeah . . . yeah," she whispered, brushing away his hand. When she was able to focus, she looked around. In other circumstances, she would have been charmed by the lovely green countryside abounding with wildflowers. But right now, Laura had other, more serious things on her mind. The car was resting at an odd angle, as if the hubcap on her side was deep in a bog. "Oh, Lord." She sighed despondently. "What have I done?"

"I'd say about a one-eighty," Devlin answered dryly.

She glanced over at him, scanning him worriedly. "Are you okay? I'm—I'm really sorry about this. I'll pay to have it fixed, of course."

He shook his head. "I don't think there's much wrong except that we're stuck."

There was a tap on Laura's window. She twisted about to see the elderly man who had been sitting on the cart. His whiskered face was drawn in concern. When she rolled down the window, he spoke, but Laura didn't understand a word. She looked to Devlin for help.

He smiled kindly at the man and said something back, equally incomprehensible. When the old man nodded, and turned to trudge away, Laura peered at Devlin. "Where's he going? What did he say?"

"He's going to get his son to help pull us out."

"What language was that?"

"Gaelic. This is a Gaeltacht area. People speak the native tongue here."

She eyed him skeptically. "And just how do you know the native tongue so well?"

He grinned at her, and she fought a dangerous melting feeling. "Dad taught Gaelic history. I told you that. He sponsored the Gaelic Language Club at the University of Chicago, and we spoke it in our home. It was a game—until now."

"Lucky you like language games," she said, grateful for his expertise.

"A leprechaun must be riding my shoulder today," he remarked with an odd quirk of his lips.

Laura shrugged it off, not wanting to get into another debate about the infernal little people he so loved to tease her with. Instead, she glanced out the window and watched the cart disappear into the distance.

"By the way, he's offered us his hospitality for the night."

She turned around to stare at him, never even having considered their situation to require such a thing. "Will it take *that* long?" she asked.

"It'll be dark before they get the car out."

There was nothing she could do, and there was no one to blame but herself. "I got us into a real mess," she whispered. "I'm sorry."

"No problem."

Hearing that same odd tone in his voice, she frowned. There was something he wasn't telling her. Wary now, she asked, "What is it you're keeping from me?"

His expression held faint amusement. "You won't like it," he cautioned.

The hair on her nape tingled with anxiety. "Won't like what?"

His look was warm, almost devouring. "Tell me," she rasped. "How bad can it be? Do we have to chop a ton of wood or plow a field or something to pay for our board?"

"Nothing so easy, Laura," Devlin said softly. "He assumed we were married, so I'm afraid we'll have to share a bed."

"How do you say in Gaelic, 'When pigs mambo'?"

A devilish look came into his eyes. "What if I promise to be good?"

Laura swallowed, unwillingly picturing how very good this man would be in bed. And that was *exactly* what he meant. He was not, in any way, shape or form talking about being "good" in the I-won't-try-anything sense of the word. He spoke more languages than English and Gaelic, the crafty bum.

Hating herself for dwelling on the idea for even a few seconds, she stammered, "You—you think I think you mean one thing, but I know what you *really* mean! You forget, Devlin, I've gotten to know you!"

Though he smiled benignly, the mischief never left his gaze. "I'd better get out and see what I can do to start getting us unstuck." He pulled open his door and stepped onto the rain-softened turf.

"I'm not sleeping with you, Devlin, and that's final!"

He dipped his head back inside. This time his expression was serious, his eyes bright with a smoldering query. "Laura, do you really think I'd do anything to hurt you?"

She blanched at the frankness in his expression and retreated even closer to the car door. With great effort, she managed to meet his gaze. "I—I don't think you'd *mean* to hurt me, Devlin," she said, her voice fragile. "But, one day. . . you'd walk away. You might be sorry, but you would. So—" she swallowed to control her quaking voice "—so—if we must share a bed tonight, promise me, *now*, promise you won't touch me?"

His blue eyes darkened with fury. "Dammit, Laura, when will you learn that I—" He stopped abruptly, muttering a crude oath. Ducking out, he slammed the door so hard the whole car shook.

7

BY THE TIME THE farmer and his strapping son had returned in a dilapidated old pickup, rain was pounding down, so the plan to extricate the car was postponed. Instead Laura found herself being wrapped in an oversize sweater that smelled like a farm animal, and deposited on her suitcase in the back of the pickup. Now she was enduring a bouncing trek down a narrow lane that Devlin had referred to as a *boreen*.

As the rain poured, Laura twisted around to look through the window into the cab of the truck. She noticed rather wistfully that there was only one seat, and that was the driver's. The other seat was missing entirely, as was the door on that side. Laura tried to content herself with the fact that there wouldn't have been much advantage in sitting in the cab, as far as staying dry went, anyway. So she, Devlin and their host's son, a young man of about twenty-one, shared the creaking truck bed.

As they silently rode, Laura pulled the hood of her sweater even farther over her head and huddled inside the voluminous garment as the drenching rain obscured the landscape.

"How are you doing?" Devlin whispered into her ear.

She shrugged. "How do I look?"

He grinned, and Laura couldn't help but be affected by the sensuality in his expression. He, too, had been loaned a sweater, but it was a pullover, and fitted him better than hers. She noted that his jeans were getting wet, presenting her with a view of long, rock-solid legs and trim hips, the rain-soaked fabric displaying bold, male attributes she would have been better off never glimpsing, considering her agitated state of mind.

Hurriedly she lifted her gaze. Even with his brown hair plastered to his head and rivulets of rain running down his face, he was devastatingly handsome.

She fidgeted, tucking her heels more tightly against the suitcase, and pulling the sweater across her doubled-up knees. She was almost completely cocooned inside the garment, and surprisingly dry.

"What is this fiber, anyway? It's very waterproof for a sweater."

"These are traditional Irish fisherman sweaters," he said. "They're made out of unwashed, oily yarn straight from the sheep."

Laura absorbed the information, then made a face. "That explains the smell."

Devlin chuckled aloud, and suddenly, she found herself giggling. Why, in the face of their miserable circumstances—jouncing in the back of a pickup in the drenching rain, their car disabled, and worst of all, the peril of their sleeping arrangements—was he still so hard to stay angry with? Darn his sexy hide!

Once they arrived at the thatch-roofed white stone cottage, surrounded by roses in a rainbow of hues, they were ushered inside by a thin woman with a weathered, kind face. Quickly they were settled before a peat fire, Devlin in dry jeans and Laura in a pair of borrowed woolen socks to replace her soaked shoes. About an hour later, after she'd stopped shivering, they were ushered into the tiny kitchen. With the family clustered around a trestle table watching and smiling, Laura and Devlin ate crusty fresh-baked bread and soft-rind cheese and drank hot, strong coffee.

At long last Laura felt warm, full and thoroughly exhausted. Since she could understand nothing of what was being said, she grew drowsy. The family engaged Devlin in light conversation, and Laura tried to appear interested. But she'd been so stressed for so long, she supposed it was catching up with her now—*of all times*. Besides, the odd tongue the Irish family was speaking had a lulling effect, and she found herself on the brink of nodding off.

Every so often, Devlin would partially rouse her by explaining something they were saying. Mainly about a relative this family had in California. But, after a while, Laura could no longer hide her exhaustion. Against her will, she found her head resting on Devlin's shoulder more often than not. Embarrassed, she scooted away, fighting the inevitable, blinking and smiling, pretending she was not a bit sleepy. Eventually the elderly woman escorted her from the room to show her the bathroom and gesture toward the loft where she and Devlin would spend the night.

Realizing she had to get some sleep, she nodded her thanks to the woman and disappeared into the tiny bath to wash and change. Ten minutes later, her cotton robe cinched tightly about her, she climbed the ladder to the loft, knowing exactly how those poor souls condemned to the guillotine must have felt. *Where was the Scarlet Pimpernel when you needed him!*

Riddled with anxiety, she scanned the place. It was not much bigger than a walk-in closet, and completely open to the living area below, except for a railing. The bed, itself, was little more than a cot. Well, maybe a few inches wider, but they would have to sleep like stacked spoons, nevertheless. That vision didn't exactly put her mind at ease.

She was still fretting about the predicament, when Devlin bounded over the top of the ladder. He was dressed in a sweat suit, but his feet were bare.

"It's warmer up here than I thought it would be," he said.

She silently agreed. The heat certainly collected near the roof. For once she wasn't the slightest bit cold. That probably meant Devlin would be hot. She cringed at the double meaning the word conjured, mentally amending to *uncomfortably warm*. All at once, she wished there was a hole the size of their rental car in the roof, because Devlin was removing his sweatshirt.

He caught her panicked look and frowned at her. "I'll leave the pants on. But it *is* hot," he whispered.

Then he crawled into bed and held up the covers in invitation. "I thought you were the sleepy one."

Seeing him lounging there, languorous and bare-chested, dismayed her. She noticed a silver chain glinting against the dark mat of his chest hair, moving with the slight rise and fall of his breathing. Flicking her nervous gaze downward, she scanned the low-slung waistband of his sweatpants, which displayed way too much of an indecent, flat belly for her peace of mind.

With a nod of his head, he coaxed, "Come on."

Suddenly the lamp that had been glowing below was extinguished, and the loft fell into darkness. Apparently Mr. and Mrs. O'Callaghan, had shuffled off to their own bed. As for the son—whose name had sounded something like "Ogan"—Laura knew nothing. Maybe he'd gone off to sleep in the barn with the sheep. At this moment, she only wished it was sheep she was getting ready to sleep with—smell and all. She figured a little straw in her hair tomorrow morning would be less of a price to pay than what might lie in store for her beneath those covers.

"Laura," Devlin whispered in the darkness. "You're stalling."

"Remember what you promised?" she challenged, uneasy.

Her answer was unbroken silence.

"Devlin!" she hissed.

Another long, waiting pause that stretched her nerves to the breaking point.

"I told you I wouldn't hurt you," he said very quietly, a vague edge apparent in his tone. "Come to bed. Do you want the O'Callaghans to think we're fighting on our honeymoon?"

"I don't care if they think—" She halted. "Our *what*? Why, you rotten liar!"

"I didn't tell them that," he murmured. "Mr. O'Callaghan assumed it. He decided we must be newlyweds or I'd have been hacked about you wrecking the car."

"And you didn't correct him, because I gather the only thing you *can't* say in Gaelic is 'I'm sorry, mister, but that woman and I are hardly even acquainted'!"

There was a pause before he muttered, "I won't lie. The idea of being on a honeymoon with you appealed to me."

"Oh? The idea *appealed* to you," she scoffed. "Well, pardon me! If the idea appealed to you, what right do I have to gripe!"

"One day we *will* be on our honeymoon," he insisted in a low, determined tone. "What the hell difference does it make if the O'Callaghans are the first to know?"

"First? Ha!" she charged under her breath. "I thought the wife was supposed to be the first to know."

"She's the *last* to know, and that's if I were having an affair. Right now, I can't even get my bride into bed."

"Maybe that's because you don't have a bride."

"Come here, dammit!"

"Well, that's so gallant, how can I re—"

She heard the squeak of springs, and then felt herself being swooped into the air and deposited roughly on the bed.

"Move over, darling," he warned. "Or I'll be forced to climb on top of you."

She scrambled away to hug the wall as he climbed in.

"I—er..." she stuttered, pulling the light covers up to her neck. "What if I have to get up in the night and go to the...uh..."

He heaved a curse-filled sigh. "Climb across, then. You can have the outside."

Wanting to get this over, she threw a leg across his torso, then as quickly as she could get her balance, an arm followed. When she was stretched across him, shifting her weight, he stirred. Laura was shocked to feel a telltale bulge brush her groin. She gasped, her limbs growing wickedly hot and weak at the intimate contact. Her traitorous body sizzled with reaction and her breath started to come in labored, uneven pants.

Before her stunned mind could tell her body to move, to slide on across, he'd encircled her with his arms, his hand skimming along her back to press her hips more deeply into his erection. "I love you, Laura," he vowed huskily. "Let me show you how good we can be together."

He rubbed seductively against her, and her mind grew clouded. With a frightening swiftness, she found herself unable to concentrate on anything other than the delightful sensations his arousal was causing. Her arms no longer pressed defensively away from the mattress, but went as limp as rags, and she relaxed against his chest. Helpless to do otherwise, she laid her cheek at his throat, pleading with infinite softness, "Devlin...oh...please...." Her throat closed as his fingers moved down and somehow found their way under her robe, under her short gown. She wore no panties, and she wondered why—suddenly *knew* why. Oh, Lord, she'd *known* this would happen when she'd made the conscious decision not to...not to..."

He groaned near her ear and uttered a sexy oath, gratified to find his way clear to explore, to delight. And so he did, his hands stroking, dipping, making her damp with need.

No longer a reluctant participant, she began to kiss his throat, reveling in the sensations he was engendering between her legs.

"Laura," he moaned, lifting his hips to turn both of them on their sides. As he did so, she opened herself fully to him. Curling her arms about his neck, she lifted her lips to meet his, welcoming his tongue with a primitive intensity she hadn't been aware she was capable of. As he caressed the deepest recesses of her mouth, his hands made her body quake with a sudden, unexpected orgasm. She cried out softly, clinging to him as her body shuddered in an excruciating, sweet climax.

The experience had been so hushed, so ethereal, she couldn't quite believe it had really happened. But she was too weak for it all to have been a dream. Her body tingled and was gloriously damp. Yet, Devlin was still clothed.

Drawing a leg tightly over his hip, she kissed him deeply again, and sighed a sigh that held a tinge of regret—but only a tinge. No woman in her right mind could regret what she'd just experienced. So, in the tradition of Scarlett O'Hara, she decided she'd worry about it tomorrow.

"Your turn," she whispered dreamily as she reached for the waistband of his pants and tugged. "Or should I say, still my turn." A soft laugh gurgled in her throat. "You were right, you sexy troublemaker, you. I want you inside me, bad—"

"We might make noise," he cautioned, amusement in his husky tone. "What would the O'Callaghans think?"

She dipped her hand beneath the fabric and encircled her objective, marveling at what a handful his erection was. "They'll think we're on our honeymoon...."

His chuckle tickled her breasts. "Mind if I ask a favor?"

She looked up into his eyes. "If I were smart, I'd say no and run in the other direction."

"Why don't you, then?" he taunted, his lips nipping along hers.

"Darned if I know," she murmured against his mouth.

After another earthshaking kiss, he drew away and pulled something from his sweatpants pocket, placing a small packet in her free hand. "A nineties ritual. Would you do the honors?"

When she realized what he'd handed her, she came up on one elbow and nuzzled her cheek to his chest. "If my hands are steady enough."

She fumbled for a second, but managed to open the plastic. Then, lifting the covers, she warmed to her task, first helping him remove his pants, then stroking and teasing as she sheathed him, enjoying the guttural sounds of his arousal.

Once again, she felt his knowing fingers explore along her exposed thigh. She lounged back, and before she knew it, he'd swept her robe and nightgown to the floor.

For a long moment, they gazed at each other as the very air around them seemed to grow charged with erotic promise. They were naked, the bed and their hair mussed. He reached out and touched her cheek and she turned to kiss his palm. They both were very aware that the delights they had shared so far were only a delectable prelude.

Laura, feeling a strange, wonderful surge of power, pressed him to the bed and straddled him. For a moment, she only teased, brushed, toyed and barely touched, but his responses set her on fire, and very soon the lustful foreplay became such a turn-on she could bear no more.

She took his hands and guided them to her buttocks. His soft laughter told her he understood what she wanted. He guided her, shifting his body to tantalize with intimate, subtle movements that incited delirious sighs until neither of them could stand the tension an instant longer.

Crazy with desire, Laura dug her nails into Devlin's shoulder and cried out an urgent, indecent plea. She was stunned to hear her own scandalous cry, but Devlin chuckled. "I thought you'd never ask, love," he whispered, thrusting upward to fill Laura with sweet, sharp stabs of pleasure that began at her core and sent shock waves of delight all the way to the tips of her fingers and toes.

With each searing plunge, she gasped and clutched at him. His large hands at her waist held her possessively, keeping her in the most exhilarating, intimate contact. He seemed to anticipate her needs, and began to move more swiftly, thrilling her. She responded in kind, and with budding delight that built to a teasing expectancy, until all at once she was sliding over the delicious brink. With a cry of release, she shuddered and quaked, her whole being humming with satisfaction. As she collapsed over him, sated and spent, she was dizzy with her newfound knowledge of how beautifully a woman can be gratified by a man. "Oh, Devlin ... I never knew it could be like this."

He held her tenderly, stroking her back and hips. "*I* did, my love," he reminded her, kissing the top of her head. "From the first time I saw you ..."

Hours later, rain pattered on the roof with a lulling, peaceful sound. The peat fire below had died, and Laura found herself snuggled within Devlin's embrace, relishing his encompassing warmth.

As she lay in his arms, listening to his even breathing, she felt a growing need to have him inside her again. She knew she must be mad. She couldn't have him on any permanent basis. But, as the hours had slipped by, and she'd pressed her cheek to his warm chest and heard the thud of his heartbeat, she had begun to dwell on a very outrageous notion.

Why cry over spilt—er—milk, so to speak? Why not enjoy her time in Ireland with Devlin? Why not have a little fling far away from home? After all, in a week— maybe a little more—he would be heading back to

Chicago and she to Tallahassee. That would automatically end the affair, wouldn't it?

Oh, yes, he'd talked a lot about love at first sight, but she wouldn't let that make her crazy. For all she knew, it could be his standard line for getting a woman into bed. No doubt it was a variation on the theme many men used to seduce women into a brief, meaningless affair. "I love you" was a cheap, overused phrase. Lots of women fell for it every night at singles bars and over candlelight dinners. The places changed, but the line remained pitifully the same.

Just because she hadn't run up against this particular love-at-first-sight ploy, didn't mean it wasn't a hot seller. Most women eventually fell for one version of a man's line or another, depending on the man and on the woman's emotional needs. It had been going on for years. Poor Maureen Renny had been just one of many....

Laura wouldn't fall for a stupid line, though. She hadn't last night, either. The men she had loved, and who'd really loved her, had ultimately failed her because of their weakness. She wouldn't leave herself open to such heartbreak again. She would *never* be that kind of fool.

Even as she turned to kiss Devlin's chest, she promised herself that he would not become important enough to hurt either her or her daughter. He might learn—had already learned—many intimate things about her, but he would not invade her most private sanctum: the fragile place in her heart that was already chipped and glued, and that wouldn't survive another blow.

So Devlin wouldn't even learn about Sally—her sweet but imperfect child. Pain had made her too circumspect to let that happen again.

He stirred and murmured sleepily, "I love you," then drew her more securely against his arousing nakedness.

She was shocked to discover she harbored such impetuous sexual yearning. As her body began to thrum with renewed desire, it grew clear that she did. It was also clear that this new, racy side of her was totally Devlin's fault—that irresistible devil with the haunted blue eyes.

As long as this unexpected wanton facet of her personality was his fault, and he was so near and so enticingly naked, why not indulge herself? Why not make the most of her short time with her tempting, temporary lover? A heady recklessness overtook her and she ran her tongue along the contour of his chest. "Show me how much you love me," she challenged, as her hands sought out a most interesting objective.

Jubilant laughter bubbled in her throat as Devlin, coming fully awake and fully aroused, took charge in a most breathtaking manner.

At daybreak, the rain stopped. In Gaelic, Devlin was informed that the ground was too soft to attempt to retrieve the car. He told her that if the weather remained dry, they might manage to pull the car out the next morning.

With nothing further to be done, Ogan offered to give them a ride into town so they could continue their search for Myrtle. After a tasty breakfast of orange juice and porridge, they were ready to go. They brought their bags, not wanting to put the young man out of his bed a second night, but as they left the cottage, Laura took one last wistful peek at the loft.

She couldn't quite pin down her emotions at that moment. She was sad yet giddy, forlorn yet breathless. She supposed she knew that leaving the loft didn't change much; they would simply take their hot affair elsewhere. Still, she knew in her heart that she would always remember the cozy haven, long after Devlin had gone back to Chicago.

As Ogan helped them from the truck bed, he said, "Luck to ye on yer search," then winked broadly. "Sure and I hope ye enjoyed me bed." With a knowing laugh, he ambled away, then turned back. "Ah, I nearly forgot. Today ye'll be findin' most town folk in the square. 'Tis Bachelor's Day. Ye might enter the contest, Devlin. It's a grand time. Though, from what I heard last night, meetin' women don't seem to be a problem fer ye."

"You—you speak English?" Laura called after him, stunned.

He lifted a conspiratorial brow. "Devlin said he'd be pleased for the practice to talk the native tongue, and you, says he, was a wee bit shy o' speaking ta strangers." The young man rolled his eyes. "I made me bed on the floor by the fire, y'know. Didn't mean to hear, but..." He grinned lewdly, and Laura wanted to die. Going on, he explained, "Me Da and Ma are simple farm folk, but fer meself, I been ta Dublin town. I know a thing or two about life. Sure and luck to ye both."

He tipped his soft-brimmed hat, then ambled off, his laughter loud and impertinent in the morning stillness.

Laura reeled around to glare daggers at Devlin. "You wanted to practice?" she echoed, her tone scathing. "Practice what! New sex positions? And that boy heard us!" She slapped out at him in her anger, but he deftly avoided her, and merely grinned.

"Don't be mad, Laura, I told you how I felt."

"But, to—to have sex with me in front of an audience!" she flared. "How could you?"

He reached for her hand, but she yanked it away.

His expression turned serious. "Laura, I had no idea he was down there."

She hated to but she did believe him. That, however, didn't make things much better. "Well...well..." she stumbled, her cheeks blazing. "Just for the record, did you get enough *practice?* Answer me, you—you manipulative jerk!"

"I didn't hear any complaints last night. Especially toward morning when you wanted to . . . practice."

Her cheeks burned as she remembered the wild ways they'd made love to each other last night. His lips, his tongue, his body had taken her places she'd never dared think of going. He'd taught her things, done things to her—uncivilized, shameless things—that made her pulse race even to recall, weakening her with renewed desire. She hated herself for the quivery way the mere vision of what they'd shared affected her, and she had trouble stifling a moan. "You're . . . you're crude," she groaned. "Go 'way and leave me alone."

He grasped her arm, blatantly disobeying her command, and steered her toward the square where town folk were milling amid tents and colorful, fluttering flags. "You love it when I'm crude," he reminded under his breath. "And, tonight, in our guesthouse room, you'll have the luxury to howl if you feel the urge. And, believe me, baby, you'll feel the urge."

Laura stumbled, her legs feeling strangely rubbery. "Don't. Don't talk like that, Devlin," she scolded.

"We're here on business. There'll be no fooling around—" She swallowed. Even she couldn't believe that, so she did the best that she could, idiot that she was, to be stern. "No fooling around until . . . until we find Myrtle."

He chuckled meaningfully. "With that kind of incentive, the woman is practically found."

At that moment, a pretty blonde bounded up to them and asked a question of Devlin in Gaelic.

Laura glanced at him in time to see his dashing grin as he nodded in response.

The girl, who Laura judged to be about twenty, giggled and wrapped a red ribbon around his left arm, above the elbow, murmuring something else in a tone that clearly indicated, "I'm available." She gave Laura a saucy look, then turned back to Devlin and spoke through another bout of giggles.

Once again he nodded and gave her a sexy grin. Laura didn't know why she cared that he was being so darned agreeable to this buxom beauty. And what in heaven's name was the red ribbon for? She noticed that the Irish girl hadn't bothered to offer *her* any ribbons.

To get Devlin's attention, Laura coughed.

He looked her way. "Just a second," he said, then turned to speak to the blonde.

Laura stiffened with resentment. *Just a second?* What was she to him all of a sudden? A piece of ratty old baggage?

The girl moved closer to Devlin. He laughed and that grated on Laura's nerves.

"Laura," Devlin said, squeezing her arm to bring her back from the black depths of her mood. "Arlene here has just claimed me for the first dance and invited me to enter the Bachelor's Day competition."

Laura was positive that her foul mood had nothing to do with jealousy. After all, he was merely a fling, a way to fulfill her sexual needs. She gulped. It was just that he could do it so well—

"Laura?" he repeated. "Did you hear me?"

She forced herself to smile pleasantly. "By all means, Devlin, who am I to stifle your...competitive impulses."

He studied her for a moment, then smiled softly. "Hell. You're jealous."

She froze in horror. That was the most ridiculous piece of nonsense she'd ever heard. Giving him a scathing look, she hissed, "Nothing of the sort, Mr. Ego Maniac. I...I was just under the impression you'd offered to help me find Myrtle."

He shrugged his broad shoulders. "We can't leave until tomorrow, anyway. Besides, with the incentive you've given me, do you think I won't find her?"

Laura eyed the grinning blonde, who had actually taken Devlin's hand and begun to tug. "Not that I care," she said shortly, "but just exactly what sort of skills does a bachelor need in order to win? I can see already you're going to do fine in the hand-holding marathon."

He grinned with pleasure. "I don't think it's my ego, Laura. You're jealous. Just wait till I get you alone, tonight."

Devlin was being tugged away toward a tent, where a lively jig had begun.

"Don't count on it," she called.

"Mill around and enjoy," he called back, clearly unconvinced by her denial. "Dance, Laura. Meet people. They can speak English. The bachelor talent show's at eight. Cheer for me."

Then he was gone. She stared after him, wondering exactly what he was planning to do tonight at the talent competition. She hadn't known him very long but she was very aware of *one* talent he had. Well, Arlene had made it clear by her smile that she wouldn't run screaming for help if the opportunity of a carnal interlude with the *talented* Devlin presented itself.

The memory of all the sexy things he could do—had done—brought on a blush. So the women of Killannin were choosing the best bachelor in town, today? Well, no matter what promises Devlin had made in the past four days, he was going to be no help at all in her search for Myrtle. With his looks, he wouldn't be left alone for one single second all day.

Good riddance, she ground out, praying she meant it. A few minutes later, she joined the growing throng, deciding she might as well start inquiring after the local population of Myrtles.

Let Devlin party hearty. Let him dance all day with every single, silly, tittering woman from miles around. Let him be the center of a swarm of eyelash-fluttering nymphs. Maybe by tonight he'd be too tired to ... to make her ... make her ...

Good Lord! What had she gotten her weak, stupid self into? Here she was in the middle of a crazy Irish festival, amid total strangers she couldn't understand. Devlin had been dragged off doing heaven-knows-what with heaven-knew-how-many...*voters!* She should be furious with him! She should never speak to him again!

So why was she standing here, all quivery and breathless, feeling her very first urge to—uh—*howl* ...?

8

LAURA SPENT THE MORNING and early afternoon wending her way through jostling crowds of friendly people as she wandered around the square and up and down the town's mile-long main street. Accompanying her along the way were the sounds of street bands. It seemed that every person with the least bit of musical talent in all of Ireland had found his or her way here to Killannin.

She found herself hard-pressed to keep from laughing as a chorus of Guinness drinkers sloshed their mugs in tipsy abandon as they stumbled across the square, bellowing an off-key Gaelic ballad at the top of their lungs. Laura had no idea what the lyrics meant, but she could tell by the gut-busting din they were creating, these festival goers harbored great sentimental support for its message. She decided the song was probably about how nice it was to get toasted in the morning and lie in an unconscious heap for the rest of the day, for that was apparently the direction in which they were headed.

Her attention was attracted to an open-sided lorry parked on the opposite flank of the grassy square. She wandered over to take a look. Seated along it, swinging their feet to the feisty rhythm, were eight musicians, whistling, drumming and fiddling a reel. A crowd of grinning and giggling school children, had gathered and were tapping their toes. Old men, their backs resting against the storefronts across the street, smoked pipes and sang with raspy voices.

The crisp air was filled with the mingled smells of frying chips, pipe tobacco, spiced Irish beef and fresh brown breads. The sun had come out, and though still cooler than Florida, it was a lovely day. This was the mildest, warmest weather Laura had experienced so far in Ireland, and she found her spirits rising with the temperature.

Maybe it was contagious—this boisterous, lively craziness that abounded around her. She tried to ignore the thought that having great sex with an astonishingly sensitive lover might have anything to do with her odd feelings of completeness, but it wasn't easy. Pushing that idea away for the hundredth time, she wandered on. Besides, where was Devlin, anyway? With *another* woman, that's where he was—with ten, maybe twenty other women. For that reason alone, she needed to push any ideas about completeness because of that man, out of her head!

She was sure he was having a ball being Mr. Stud one night, and then Mr. Available the next day. He had seemed less haunted today, less overwhelmed by his mysterious tragedy. She was sure part of his lightened mood was the fact that he'd made a successful conquest. Something like that would never fail to lift a man's spirits. And of course, the excess of female attention today couldn't hurt.

She supposed she should feel good that this Bachelor's Day thing was helping him forget whatever had brought him to Ireland, so lost and sad. After all, they were *both* benefiting from their fling, weren't they? And they'd both go their merry ways soon enough, wouldn't they? Why begrudge the man a little fun? She'd have to work on loosening up her attitude. She felt strangely possessive about Devlin right now. Of course, she'd never been in a position before where the man she slept with was nothing more than a convenience—no strings, no commitments, no apologies. It might take a little work to remember that, but for her own good, and for Sally's good, she would manage.

The main activity of the Bachelor's Day festival was in the center of the town square where the dancing tent was set up, and where single girls from surrounding hamlets had come to cavort with the region's bachelors. She'd overheard, from a smattering of conversations, that more than a few marriages resulted from this festival. And for today's lucky winner, there was the *International* Bachelors Festival in Ballybunion, County Kerry, in September.

The title of International Bachelor of the Year didn't necessarily have to go to an Irishman just because it was held here, for Americans entered every year. She sighed, picturing Devlin crowned with the title. His winning such an honor wasn't difficult to imagine. The man had an almost-intimidating male presence, with those massive shoulders, that lean body and those powerful, sinewy legs. And that smile—it was scandalous, the effect it had on a woman. She ought to know. . . .

Yes, she could see Devlin Rafferty as the International Bachelor of the Year, damn his gorgeously male hide. Unable to help herself, Laura wondered how he might be doing. If he was even still in the running. She hadn't seen any of the ribbon-wearing bachelors being tossed out of town on their backsides, so she figured the Killannin festival rules had nothing so formal as semifinal or final rounds. Clearly this was a ripsnorting, go-all-out-all-day flirt fest—winner take all.

She'd heard—in snickering whispers—that the winner would have no shortage of pretty colleens' attentions once the contest was over. Apparently there was a sexual side-benefit to winning, and any wild frolicking that went on in private, after the king was crowned, didn't affect his eligibility for the upcoming international contest. Such seemed to be the way with contests, she thought grudgingly. Women had to remain—at least publicly—above the appetites of the flesh while men were practically penalized if they did.

High-pitched laughter drew Laura toward the entrance to the big tent, where Devlin was sure to be reveling for all he was worth. She peeked inside, not because she was the least bit interested in what Devlin might be doing, *certainly*. Yet there was every possibility that Myrtle *might* be among the partying horde that seemed to be growing bigger by the minute.

A quaint assortment of musicians on a wooden platform provided the wild, jigging music. She recognized some of the instruments. Two violins, which she'd learned were termed "fiddles" by the locals, a flute, an accordion and a couple of tambourines that looked rather odd by American standards. One nice young man had been kind enough to explain in English that the instruments were called *bodhrán*, and were covered in goatskin. He'd added that the *bodhrán* were capable of making the dead rise up and dance when played properly. The band members ranged in age from a thin teenage boy in coveralls and hobnail boots to a wizened old man clad in a spiffy tweed jacket and bow tie, who looked to be about five hundred years old. He was squeezing and pulling on an accordion, and the agonized expression on his toothless face made him appear as though each yank and squeeze would be his last on earth. But he survived, apparently thriving as the music took on a life of its own, growing into a spirited stomping, hooting, roaring string of diddley-diddley-dees.

Dancers whooped and laughed as they whirled by, their feet dancing to the age-old Gaelic rhythms. Laura found herself clapping and swaying left and right as the jangling brew of high and low pitches swept her away with its exuberance.

She finally spotted Devlin, who was taller than most men in the tent, and appeared every so often. Against her will, Laura found herself craning to see him as he reeled around on the wooden planks. With his legs and hips encased in his snug jeans, it took no great effort to notice the sexy coil of muscle straining against denim, revealing strong thighs and calves as he leaped and turned, his booted feet flashing in concert with his partner's and everyone else's on the floor.

He moved with such surefooted grace, it was clear that his father had not only sponsored the Gaelic Speaking Club at whatever university he'd taught at, but also the Irish Dirty Dancing Society, for Devlin was no novice, and was plainly favored among the not-too-subtle single women whirling around him.

It was foolish, she knew, but she had a feeling she could actually hear his deep, rich laughter amid the cacophony of noise. What a ridiculous notion. And just as foolishly she thought that he'd actually seen her—picked her out of the milling crowd of nearly two hundred people dancing, wandering through or watching. How silly.

But she felt it—a heat that lingered around her like a caressing cloak—and it made her tingle. With a shake of her head, she tried to convince herself how idiotic that was. But no matter how she tried, she was unable to take her eyes from the dizzying panorama on the dance floor—and most especially, one tall American's rakish grin as he charmed the women of Killannin.

Laura noticed that Devlin changed partners often. That was one of the very few rules. No bachelor could dance with the same woman twice during the same hour. And no bachelor could have a meal with *fewer* than five single women at once. Five women? Obviously a panel of bachelors had made up that rule! Laura harrumphed aloud.

"Did ye speak ta me, miss?"

She turned away from the tent to see a man of about her own height wearing a soft wool cap and a blue knit sweater. He had a red mustache and sparkling green eyes. It came to her only after a few dumbstruck seconds that he'd actually spoken to her in English.

"How did you know I couldn't speak Gaelic?" she asked, deciding he seemed a nice-enough sort.

He laughed. "Ah, sure and a Yank sticks out in a small Irish town. Are ye here for the festival or just passin' through?"

"I'm actually here on business."

"Ye don't say, now. And what might that be, if I might inquire?"

"I'm looking for a woman named Myrtle." Laura found herself having to speak up for the music and the dancers were growing noisier as the players escalated the tempo. "I haven't had much luck—not speaking Gaelic, and all."

"Myrtle, ye say?" he shouted back. "She be kin?"

"No. I've never met her. Do you live here?"

He nodded. "Aye. These twenty-five years."

She smiled at him. He didn't look that old. "I notice you don't have on a ribbon," she commented loudly so that she could be heard over the clamoring sounds around them.

"'Tis a pity, but there'll be none o' that competing fer me," he shouted with a hearty laugh. "Me wife of three weeks, says she, she'd cut out me poor heart if I give a kind eye to any pretty colleen." He shrugged his narrow shoulders. "Sure and she'll no doubt have me heart anyway, for passin' the time with a beauty such as yerself."

Laura flushed, and changed the subject back to business. "Do you know of a woman named Myrtle who lives here? She'd probably be in her fifties or sixties, but I'm afraid I don't know her last name. Her maiden name was Renny, though."

He twitched his mustache, a movement Laura noticed he seemed to favor each time he planned to speak. "Myrtle, ya say?" His red eyebrows came together in consideration. "There's no Myrtle Renny, but there be a Myrtle Moody. I'd figure her ta be near the proper age."

Laura perked up. "Where could I find her?"

"Sure and I couldn't say, right off, ya know, it bein' festival day." He inclined his head in the direction of a crooked footpath that led from the main road behind a crumbling wall into some woods. "The Moody cottage be down past the churchyard amongst a grove of linden trees, by a wee stream." He pointed, then motioned off to his left. "Mind, if ye make the natural bridge, you've gone too far."

She nodded and yelled, "Thank you, uh . . ." She'd never asked him his name.

He smiled and twitched his mustache. "Brian Murphy. And yer name would be?"

"Laura Todd," she said. "Thank you, Brian."

"Yer more 'an welcome, Miss Laura Todd from America. And may the doctor never earn a pound on ye or yer loved ones."

Laura smiled at him and nodded her thanks, then headed away from the noisy square. She hoped this short walk along a woodland path would be the end of her job here. So far, these past four days—almost five— had been a great deal more stressful than she'd ever imagined they could be. She'd certainly *never* dreamed she'd become involved in a sexual interlude with a virtual stranger in the bargain.

The sounds of the festivities began to diminish as she strolled along the path. A sparkle to her left drew her gaze to a silent stream, and she found herself slowing her pace, enjoying the wood with its sheltering darkness, its soul-calming quiet and restful beauty. Inhaling deeply, she detected the delicate scents of heather and hawthorn, and though new smells to her, she'd learned to recognize them in the brief time she'd been in Ireland. She heard a *plop* and realized a fish had jumped in the stream.

She wandered closer, weaving through the trees until she was standing directly beside the stream. The water was so clear, she could see fish shimmering by, flashing and zigzagging.

Off in the distance, she could still hear the merry-making from the dancing tent. Feeling a flash of foolish jealousy, she muttered, "I hope you get blisters, Mr. Rafferty!"

"Now is that nice, when I've come all this way with news?"

Laura jumped a foot at the unexpected sound of Devlin's voice. There he was, lounging against the trunk of an oak, watching her with those wickedly seductive eyes.

She found herself nervously floundering before the power of his gaze and the daunting sexuality that he exuded. "I— Where did you come from?" she finally managed, sounding steadier than she felt. "I thought you were back there doing the wild thing, Irish-style. What did they do, disqualify you for unsanctioned pelvic thrusts?"

His grin was devilish. "Now, what would make you think of a thing like thrusts?" he teased, his knowing tone prompting a rush of warmth to her cheeks. Devlin knew darned good and well where the idea had come from. And because of her rash remark, he was armed with the knowledge that she hadn't been able to put what they'd shared last night out of her mind.

Desperately wanting the subject changed, she forced herself to stare him directly in the eye. "So what's the news that was so important it would drag you away from your flock of eager maidens?"

"It's about Myrtle Moody," he said.

"You found her?"

He stretched out a hand, taking her fingers in his. "I'll show you."

She had no idea why she was allowing herself to be tugged along, this way. Devlin had some weird power over her that short-circuited her ability to protest. So hand in hand, they walked through the cool glade.

She peeked over at him. He seemed to sense her perusal, glancing her way, his smile warm. "Are you having a good time?" he asked finally as they walked.

She looked away. "Just dandy." Her gaze drawn back against her better judgment, she asked, "Did you drop out of the contest or something?"

He laughed that same, recognizable laugh that made her tingle. "No. All the contestants get some time to themselves." He winked, his grin wry. "You know. Commune with nature, so to speak."

She got it. "And you decided to spend your washroom break with me. How charming."

"I knew you'd be pleased."

"I suppose you must be aware of the fact that I was already on my way to Myrtle Moody's house when you caught up with me."

"I gathered that."

She stared at him, perturbed. "And I suppose you intend to take the credit for finding her when we get there?"

"Actually, Laura—" he drew her around to face him, his expression sober, masculine intent sparking in his eyes "—I've already been there, and I already know all you're going to find out today." Dragging her close, he held her to him, rubbing his body suggestively against her, murmuring, "The truth? I wanted to be near you— very near you—for a little while. Tonight's so damned far away."

Dizzy and stunned, she could do little more than indulge in the sensations his arousal was stirring to life inside her. Devlin knew how to touch a woman, how to fill her with need and desire, even when he was fully clothed. Their hips rocked and massaged in a wanton, uncivilized waltz, and she swayed with him, harboring no regard for propriety or the right or wrong of making love right here, right now, in these woods. His gaze seared her with an unspoken vow of utter rapture.

"Oh, Devlin," she whispered plaintively, the last vestiges of rationality draining quickly away. "We—we can't. We aren't going to make love here...."

His hand slid easily inside the waistband of her slacks, then down to caress boldly between her legs. "Tell me you don't want me, and we won't."

She opened her lips, but no words came. Nothing formed there but a quivery smile. Closing her eyes, she exulted in the man and his erotic gifts. Clutching at him, straining to bring him in more intimate contact as her fever grew, she lifted her lips, seeking the exquisite touch of his. A needy moan escaped her throat as his mouth found hers. With his lips urgent and ravenous against hers, he drew her down to their bed of sweet, cool grasses in the shadowy wood.

LAURA SNUGGLED IN THE crook of his arm. Once again, they had shared marvelous, uncomplicated sex, and she was still drugged with its afterglow. Because she had grown chilly, Devlin had helped her dress, trailing warm, sweet kisses over her skin as he proceeded.

Now they were both clothed, but in no hurry to leave the refuge where they had indulged in wild, uninhibited pleasure. Laura held him tightly to her, recalling everything in a rosy haze. She sighed again, arching up to graze his chin with a kiss.

"Why are you sighing, darling?" he asked softly.

She kissed him once more, and he lowered his face to meet her lips in a tender, heart-stopping response as he gathered her close.

Once the kiss ended, he repeated, "Why the sighs?"

She looked up at the tree branches above them and smiled. "I don't know. I guess I just wish we could stay here forever and not think about tomorrow."

He chuckled and she felt it all the way to her toes. "Oh, no, you don't. I want to make love to you in a lot of different places. But," he added, running his hand along her inner thigh, "I wouldn't mind another taste of your passion right here. If you think you have the energy."

His fingers were arousing her again, and she leaned back to enjoy his ministrations, emptying her mind of everything—of the future, of her worrisome mix of emotions involving this man. She didn't want to think right now. . . .

"I see you're interested," he murmured, nipping and tickling the sensitive area of her ear with his questing tongue. "Oh, Devlin," she responded in a faint cry. "You're so bad. . . ."

He laughed, dipping his hands into intimate places, stealing Laura's wits with deliciously wanton advances. "Am I really that bad?"

"Mmm," she moaned, licking her lips as she began to writhe with delight. "Oh, Devlin . . . You're so good. . . ."

A SHORT TIME LATER, having regained some measure of rationality, Laura sat staring down at the man who could do things to her that must be classed as either the *best* that had ever happened to her or the *worst!*

He lay there, smiling up at her, the satisfied male of the species. She knew she was foolish, but found her silly female-of-the-species-self smiling back. "I'm afraid you've broken one of the big rules of Bachelor's Day, Mr. Rafferty," she admonished, her stern tone failing miserably.

He grinned wickedly, taking her hand and kissing the palm. His tongue danced against it, and she shyly withdrew, afraid she would weaken again and topple onto him yet again. She must put a stop to this absurd "lust spree," right now! They were lucky they hadn't been caught so far. Spending any more time rolling around in the woods could be risky.

"Devlin, really," she scolded. "You're an animal." Abruptly she stood, then swayed dizzily. Before she could either right herself or fall flat on her face, he was standing beside her, steadying her.

"Are you okay?" he asked.

She smiled wanly. "It's nothing a couple of years in a convent wouldn't fix."

He kissed the top of her head and lifted a blade of grass from her tangled curls. "Come on. We'd better go."

She leaned against his solid strength as they began to walk.

"Do you know what Killannin means?" he asked gently.

"I didn't know it meant anything." She was glad for his support, for her legs were unsteady.

"It has a very definite meaning." He held her close, rubbing her arm as they strolled. "I'll give you a hint. It has something to do with what we did this afternoon."

She glanced over at him, skeptical. "Killannin is Gaelic for *great sex?*"

He laughed, squeezing her tenderly. "Close."

"Okay. Then it must mean *horny guy in the woods*."

"I beg your pardon," he mocked through a chuckle. "I wasn't alone back there. And *I* wasn't the one begging for me to—"

"Okay, okay!" she blurted, her cheeks suddenly ablaze. "So, what *does* Killannin mean?"

His arm slid down to capture her hip and stroke seductively as he turned her to him, his lips feather-touching hers with tempting persuasion. "It means..." He kissed her softly, lingeringly, and Laura found herself savoring every second. After too short a time, he released her, and reluctance flooded through her as he moved slightly away. "Killannin means *Lovers' Wood*," he explained huskily.

She blinked. "Really?"

There was a hedonistic glint in his eyes. "Works for me. How about you?"

Unable to help herself, a low-pitched laugh gurgled in her throat. He was such a scamp and a tease. Playfully, she reached down to fondle a particularly skilled portion of his anatomy, assuring him, "Oh, Devlin, it works very, very well."

"Tonight," he vowed against her hair, "you howl...."

Laura shivered with anticipation, knowing she was completely insane, but loving every insane minute of it.

"And now the bad news—about Myrtle Moody," he said, taking her hand and aiming her along the path again.

She stiffened at the sudden reminder of why she was there and where she'd been headed when she'd been so—staggeringly interrupted. The reality check made her flinch. Where had her competent, efficient professionalism gone? Darn Devlin and his talented—

Gulping, she shot a worried glance at him and in a frail voice, echoed, "Bad news?"

9

MYRTLE'S BUNGALOW was tiny and white with yellow trim. Even its wooden steps were painted yellow. Saffron window boxes were filled to overflowing with diminutive red roses interspersed with lacy fingers of ivy that spilled down the sides and shivered in the breeze. A fluttering piece of white paper was tacked to Myrtle's yellow door.

She walked close enough to see what was written there and grew dismayed. "It's in Gaelic," she moaned. "I hope it says she's gone to her belly-dancing lesson and she'll be back in fifteen minutes."

Devlin squeezed her fingers and gave her a sympathetic look. "More like two days."

"Oh, that's just fine," she mumbled.

"It says here, she's gone off to buy supplies. From the note, I gather she earns her living making handwoven tweed jackets."

"Does it say where she is?" Laura asked hopefully.

"Afraid not. But now that you have her last name, you can call her in a couple of days."

"I suppose." She sighed despondently. "I was hoping we'd put an end to this mystery today."

Laura felt a surprise kiss, and looked at Devlin's grinning face. "Might as well go back to the festival," he suggested. "Nothing for you to do here."

She shook her head at him. He was incorrigible. "Oh?" she goaded. "Now that you've had your—shall we say—break, you're ready to go back and be the center of female attention again?"

"I love it when you're jealous," he teased, exasperating her by looking so appealing and so sure of himself.

Her body still glowing from his lovemaking, she couldn't conjure up any real irritation, but managed to pull her hand from his. "Your ego could sink ships, Mr. Rafferty," she retorted. "The Navy should hear about you!"

Turning on her heel, she began to walk back along the path toward Killannin. "Rush on ahead, Devlin," she called over her shoulder. "I'm sure Arlene or whatever her name is, is pining away, wondering where you've gone."

"Very funny." He caught up, taking her arm. "If I intend to win, though, we shouldn't be seen walking together—alone."

"Well, I certainly wouldn't want to be the cause of your losing the crown on my account, Mr. Have-Sex-In-The-Woods-And-Leave-'Em." Again she pulled free and hurried on ahead. "By all means, be on your merry way."

He laughed, his long strides easily keeping pace with her. "If I win, do you know what the prize is?"

She shrugged. Somehow this conversation wasn't as funny as it had been at the start. Maybe recalling him twirling around that tent clasping first one fawning woman and then another, bothered her more than she'd let on, even to herself. "The grand prize is of no interest to me. I presume it'll put you in some sort of international finals, and for the next several months, you'll have carte blanche with the ladies of Ireland." Well aware of what sort of pleasure he had the ability to give, she felt a surge of envy, adding under her breath, "I presume you came over here partly to get laid, so I'm *thrilled* for you."

"To get—"

She felt a grip on her arm, strong enough to drag her around to face him. His mouth set, he stared at her, and she found it nearly impossible to look him in the eye. When he spoke, his words were measured and hard-edged: "So you've caught on to my deep, dark master plan. That's very good. You should give psychic readings."

She wrenched away, knowing she'd said an unkind thing, but her this-is-just-a-fling-and-I-mustn't-get-possessive attitude kept sliding to the back of her mind. Old habits about love and commitment were hard to kill.

"Look," she said earnestly, wanting to make amends. "Your reasons for doing what you do are none of my business. You're a nice guy. You're good-looking. You've been unhappy. We both have. And we've both had a little . . . fun together. But I don't own you and I certainly don't *want* to own you."

As she spoke, she noticed his jaw had tightened and his gaze had grown icy, but she forged ahead: "Go on back to your Bachelor's Day contest and have a good time." She felt a flash of guilt and added, "And—uh, thanks for your help translating. I don't know what I'd have done without you."

He stood there looking flawlessly sexy, watching her with hooded eyes. After a moment, he flashed a crooked grin. "Hell, darling," he chided, "I'm glad I could be of *service*." Without another word, he struck off through the woods toward the festivities.

She stared after him, her stomach twisting in a knot. Her only excuse was that her stupid emotions were starting to get tangled up with the man. What was wrong with her? She was a woman of the nineties, for heaven's sake. As long as a woman was sexually responsible, she ought to be able to sleep with a man without getting all involved. It wasn't Devlin's fault that she was having trouble separating good, clean sex from all her old, outmoded ideas about everlasting love and "meaningful relationships."

After a hard-fought internal battle, Laura made a decision that would patch things up with Devlin and salve her conscience, as well. Tonight, after the contest, she'd apologize—very persuasively—and all would be well. She'd learn this nineties thing, yet. If she planned to keep Sally's handicap from causing any more trauma in either Sally's life or her own, she'd have to learn to be blasé about having sex with a drop-dead desirable man.

Blasé! That was the word. From now on, Laura Todd was going to have a meaningless little escapade in Ireland and be utterly, utterly blasé about sex with Devlin Rafferty, the ultimate bachelor stud of Killannin!

DEVLIN WAS ROYALLY hacked when he'd stomped off. The rest of the afternoon, he'd spent being chattered at by local women he cared nothing about, and his face had grown sore from faking a smile. *Damn Laura.* What was this "I don't want to own you" crap? He'd thought, once they'd made love, she'd see the truth of what he'd been saying all along—that they were meant for each other. And now, today, after blowing his mind again out there in the woods, and snuggling up against him and practically purring like a kitten, she still har-

bored the absurd notion they wouldn't spend the rest
of their lives together, raising a family and making wild
love? He'd been so floored and angry by what she'd
said, he couldn't say much in reply, and had left.

Besides, he needed the prize money. It was the
equivalent of almost five hundred bucks. For a man
without a job or prospects for one, he could use the
money. Apparently Laura had no idea how much cash
was involved.

It was after nine o'clock, and the talent contest was
in full swing. Devlin sat with the other bachelors,
waiting his turn to perform. At the moment, Ogan was
up there doing a heavy-footed jig. The audience seemed
to be enjoying it, hooting and clapping to the thud,
clank and squeak of the band's accompaniment.

Devlin scanned the people packing the tent. Laura
wasn't there. Since sunset came late in Ireland in May,
there was still plenty of activity in the square, so he
supposed she could be enjoying any manner of musical entertainment along the street. He'd hoped she'd
have been interested enough to watch him perform. It
was fairly clear, now, that he'd been wrong.

Those watching the competition were all sitting on
blankets. And some of the children were managing to
sleep, even amid the clamor of the band and Ogan's
flying, clomping boots.

After a few final not-so-surefooted steps, a last leap-
ing half turn with elbows flailing and shoulders wagging, Ogan came to a halt and gave a loose-limbed bow.
He was rewarded with a round of applause that would
have rivaled anything Fred Astaire had ever received.
Devlin smiled. Ogan was plainly one of Killannin's favorite sons.

Even though Ogan had given them a bit of teasing this morning, Devlin had spoken with him enough today to be sure he'd never banter around the risqué tidbit about hearing Laura and him making love. Devlin didn't mind so much for himself, but he hated to think of Laura as the brunt of embarrassing looks. He hadn't meant to cause her upset, dammit. He'd only wanted to love her.

A lot of good *that* had done him. She'd made it clear this afternoon that she didn't want to make any promises or hear any. She wanted nothing more complex than a sexual outlet, and Devlin had come along at a time when she'd been vulnerable. She was fighting the commitment demands he was making with the best weapons she had—denial and harsh words. Okay, if uncomplicated sex was what she thought she needed, then by damn, that's what she would get. He could play that game if she insisted on it. If she couldn't cope with the idea of love and "forever," he'd go along with this no-strings-attached farce if it made her feel less threatened. For a while, at least . . .

Hearing his name called, Devlin stood, grinned his fake smile again, and bounded up the steps to the platform to join the band. When he did, he was startled by the squeals that came from a host of women gathered in the tent.

Leaning over to shout instructions to the elderly man at the accordion, he made a sudden decision to sing an old Irish lullaby his father used to sing to him when he was a little boy. The ballad was subdued and wistful. Its lyrics told of misty mornings, of quiet green valleys and waves crashing against cliffs. There was a haunting blend of beauty and bleakness in the melody. And in its verses lay the strength, sorrow and spirit that was

Ireland: a land these people loved, a land his father and
mother had loved. And it was the land where he had
found *his* love—Laura Todd. One day, he vowed to sing
this lullaby to his children—his and Laura's children.
He nodded for the music to begin.

The band started to play. Onlookers grew hushed,
clearly recognizing the tune. When, at last, the subdued prelude ended, Devlin began to sing.

LAURA STOOD JUST OUTSIDE the tent, watching the horizon. Dusk was beginning to darken the sky. To her
astonishment, there were still no threatening rain
clouds. What an un-Irish day this had been, with its
cheerful warmth and even more cheerful people—from
what she'd been able to understand of them, that is.
She'd had a dinner of some sort of chowder in the
guesthouse where they were registered. It had been
quite good. All the while, she'd been entertained by a
street fiddler who'd taken a liking to her. It had been
quite a problem to convince the man that she wasn't in
the market for a boyfriend who played the fiddle. But,
finally, he'd gotten the message and taken off after a
pretty redhead.

While she was preoccupied by the fiddler, Devlin was
eating dinner with a bevy of Irishwomen. As she'd
walked by a pub, she'd heard his deep laughter, and
hadn't been able to keep herself from stopping and
staring inside. When he'd seen her standing there, his
expression had changed to one of—she couldn't tell
quite what. His lips had lingered in the semblance of a
smile as he'd silently regarded her. But all too quickly,
one of his admirers had taken his arm and said something, and he'd turned away to answer.

Laura quickly left. And now, she didn't quite know why she was lingering out here on the grass by the tent. She supposed she was curious about Devlin's "talent." Well, she didn't have to be curious anymore. She'd heard the squealing as his name had been shouted a moment ago, and she'd realized how stiffly, how anxiously, she'd been anticipating this.

As soon as he began to sing, she knew what she'd known all day but hadn't wanted to think about. Devlin Rafferty was going to win the whole dratted thing! Lord, the man could do everything. He could speak Gaelic. He could dance reels and jigs as though he'd done them every day of his life. He could make love like—

She bit her lip. She'd thought she'd been mentally reciting his talents where *Ireland* was concerned. She'd *meant* to add that he could also sing in Gaelic. He had a voice that sounded like a love-song-crooning Elvis Presley, if Elvis had been blessed with a rich Irish brogue.

Reluctantly, she made her way to the tent's entrance, not sure why she had to actually see him. He certainly didn't have to be seen to be believed. His performance had such unearthly beauty, she felt herself shiver in response, even though she had no idea what the words meant.

Yet for some demented female reason, she had to see, had to watch. She sensed that years from now, she'd think back fondly on this moment, about this whole interlude in her life, and—as irrational as that might be—she would smile.

She peeked inside the tent, then slipped in, plastering herself to the back canvas wall. Devlin's baritone voice filled the air. She noticed that the listeners appeared to be in awe. One or two were even dabbing at tears. When she glanced his way again, she was stunned to realize he was watching her. She could only stare back, caught up in his remarkable, melodic spell.

He continued to watch her, but he didn't smile. Yet, as he sang, his expression reflected a sweep of emotions—passion, torment and enduring warmth. Though she was too far away to be sure, she had a feeling that there was also pain in his eyes—that old pain she'd seen so often over the past few days. For some reason, she felt that pain more readily at this moment than she'd ever felt it before.

She wanted to turn away. To carelessly walk away would have been better; it would have helped prove what she'd said this afternoon—that she didn't want to own him. But she couldn't ignore the virile, yet somehow vulnerable, image he presented now, or the velvety sound of his voice—not until the last note melted away into the cool evening air. When the audience began to applaud, she came out of her stupor, and spun around to escape from the tent.

Maybe she just needed a little space, some time to be by herself and regain a degree of detachment. Later, she'd meet him in her room, after he'd accepted his prize, whatever that was. She'd apologize for this afternoon, and they'd make crazy, awesome love. That would be the beginning and the end of that. Men were easy to appease. A tumble between the sheets usually took care of any little disagreements. She hadn't had very much experience in that area, but men were men. They were basically simple creatures, after all.

Before he could get back to the guesthouse and find her, however, she would call Sally and the Dingle Bay Country House to see if there were any messages from her boss. As she scurried along the main street, she tried to discount the nagging feeling that she might be using Devlin for her own sexual purposes. She shook it off. He didn't really think she was the *only* woman in the world for him. Where had her savvy gone? Her single-businesswoman knowledge of single businessmen? Of course, it was a line. Granted. It was a good line, and he was extremely good at it. Probably it got him a lot of bedroom mileage. Just as long as *she* remained clear and rational on the subject. That was the important thing.

Laura went into the guesthouse and climbed the steps to their adjoining rooms, shocked to find herself tingling with anticipation. Tonight was the night she would howl. Devlin—who was being crowned Killannin's most eligible bachelor—had promised. . . .

LAURA SQUINTED AT HER travel alarm again, unable to believe what she saw. It was five o'clock in the morning, and Devlin had never come back. She had long since lost the mood to make love with him. Right now, she was just about as angry as any woman could be who'd ever thought she was going to get to howl and had been carelessly stood up—*stood up in bed!* That had to be almost as humiliating as being left waiting at the church. Not quite, maybe, but only because it wasn't as public. But she was humiliated, nevertheless.

How dare he! How dare he make love to her in that cottage loft and then again yesterday afternoon in the woods, and now, stay out all night long with heaven knew how many Irish sexpots? Well, it would be a *desperate* day in hell before he'd have the chance to make her howl. No matter how much she might have anticipated it, wanted it, even hoped for it, she *had* her pride. And Devlin Rafferty would not come home from a night of carousing with every hot-to-trot local wench and then expect her to simply fall into his horny arms.

Just then, she heard a key rattle in a lock, and she found herself stiffening with expectancy in spite of her outrage. She wanted to give herself a sound lecture, but she couldn't. All her thoughts were focused on the sound at the door.

When the rattling died away, the door didn't open. *It didn't open.*

After a tense minute, Laura realized she'd been holding her breath, and shakily inhaled. When she had her breath back, she also realized with a mixture of disappointment and anxiety and pure fury, that Devlin had gone into his own room. She heard a giggle, then a second, higher-pitched laugh. A woman? *Two women?* Devlin was with *two* women?

She was stunned by the truth of it, and it hurt as badly as if he'd slammed her in the stomach with a brick. Devlin was taking several of the local women to his bed. He'd been out all night with all manner of females, and now he was bringing a group of them back here, to his room. Right next to hers. Furthermore, he planned on spending the rest of the night making another woman—several other women—good Lord! The word *howl* rushed into her consciousness. She couldn't stand to say it, couldn't stand to think it. Instead, she flipped roughly onto her stomach and pulled her pillow over her head. She'd be damned if she'd listen. *Damn!*

Damn Devlin Rafferty!

Damn all single men and their infernal lines!

Damn this uncomplicated, no-strings-sex-in-the-nineties thing!

DEVLIN KNEW HE WAS in for it when he saw Laura eating her breakfast alone. She tossed him one brief glance—or rather, one deadly glare—and went back to stirring brown sugar into her porridge. He smiled to himself. She was angry. Good. She may have thought she didn't want to own him, but that's not the message she'd flashed with her eyes. She was hurt and furious that he hadn't returned to her bed last night.

That, my little Laura, is a taste of the good old one-night-stand-let's-play-house life-style, he informed her mentally. If she wanted to be in a completely free, no-commitment relationship, then she would naturally expect him to have other women, and he would naturally expect her to have other men.

Of course, he didn't give a damn about having other women, and it had taken all his persuasive powers to convince Arlene and Fenella to come back to his room for no other reason than to teach them to play a poker game called Between the Sheets. He'd chosen that game, figuring he could use its suggestive name to infuriate Laura, which was exactly what he hoped she'd be—infuriated and jealous enough to realize she loved him.

"Morning," he said cheerfully as he slid into the chair opposite her. "Sleep well?"

She didn't lift her gaze to meet his, but he noticed she hesitated with her spoon an inch from her lips, as though she wanted to say something but thought better of it. He tried again, "How's the porridge?"

She swallowed, then took a sip of her coffee, obviously stalling.

"Laura?" he prodded. "Anything wrong?"

After a couple of false starts at taking a bite, she put her spoon down. Her lashes fluttered upward and she met his gaze, then looked away again, as though even the briefest eye contact was abhorrent to her. "I'm not talking to you," she muttered. "Go away and never speak to me again, you, you . . ."

She said something he couldn't quite make out, but he was certain it was nothing she'd learned in Sunday school. "I didn't quite catch that," he urged, amused by her discomfort.

She had taken up her spoon again, but at his remark she thumped it back down and shot him a blazing scowl. "Do not make me repeat what I said," she whispered thinly. "I might singe some of your most precious body parts, and we wouldn't want to blunt your—your nocturnal pursuits, now would we!"

He gave her one of his most aboveboard expressions, as though he had no idea what could be bothering her. "Do I detect a note of petulance in your attitude this morning?"

"No," she retorted, then took a deep breath, clearly attempting to appear casual. "No, Devlin, don't be silly." She laughed aloud, a meager, counterfeit attempt that fooled no one within hearing. "I—I just don't think this is the place to discuss the chapter meeting of the local ménage-à-trois society, that's all." She clenched her jaw, appearing to fortify herself, then glared indignantly at him. "I don't want to discuss it," she said in a voice that was so tight it was barely audible. "Let's just say, with the sort of—of *contact sports* you enjoy, I—I simply don't want you around anymore!"

He leaned forward, resting his forearms on the table so that his hands were very near hers. Instantly, she yanked her fists into her lap. That retreat did nothing to deter his smile. "Yes, you do, Laura," he insisted, his tone low and seductive. "You want me. You know it and I know it."

She gaped at him. It was plain she was incredulous that he would make a bold innuendo mere minutes after leaving a duo of the local women sexually sated up in his bed. He wanted to laugh, but restrained himself.

Obviously, his plan was paying off. He'd had plenty of time to work it out during the *craic*, as the locals called the hours of pub-hopping celebration surrounding the winning bachelor. Throughout all the well-wishing and merrymaking, dancing and hilarity, the idea had come to him.

Hell, since his winning required his presence for the final round of festivities in his honor, he'd decided he might as well get some benefit out of being away from Laura. He'd use this time to force her into a reality check of sorts—to face how she really felt about him. It was a gamble, but he hoped she would see things in a different light after last night. The toughest part had been keeping Arlene and Fenella in their clothes. And it had been a strain to keep them giggling and squealing loud enough to ensure that Laura would get the idea he wanted her to get. But her dismayed expression told him she had.

"You, Devlin Rafferty, are the forty shades of green scum that forms on stagnant Irish ponds," she hissed. "I heard you skulk in this morning at five o'clock, drunk, with your brigade of Irish bimbos. Don't try to deny it."

He'd been waiting for this, practically begging for it. "I wasn't drunk," he corrected with mock indignation. "And there were only two young ladies with me. But who's counting?"

Laura's golden-brown eyes widened, as though aghast that he admitted the whole sleazy business to her face. She gulped several times, seemingly at a loss for words.

He looked up as his waitress arrived, who by *no* freak chance was Fenella. She whispered a few Gaelic words as she set his breakfast of bacon, eggs and orange juice before him, tittering delightedly when he patted her hand in appreciation. After the rosy-cheeked redhead had wiggled off, he commented, "I've always been partial to Irish bacon. How's your porridge?"

She gawked at him. "Only *two*?" she echoed in a strangled voice. "*Only two!* Is that all you have to say? You bring two women up to your room for sex, and you act like it's normal? What was I, a slow night?"

In a calculated, relaxed maneuver, he took up his fork and sampled his scrambled eggs and grilled tomatoes, before murmuring truthfully, "Laura, I would never consider making love with you a slow night."

He took another bite, not tasting anything, his body vibrating with the need to tell her the truth, take her in his arms, smother her with kisses, and prove to her once again that he loved her more than his own life. But he didn't do it. He'd found out the hard way that if he did, she'd run like a frightened doe. So he merely ate, mechanically, noticing nothing of the savory flavor of the bacon. He ate and waited. A cold, forbidding eternity dragged by.

"Am I supposed to be flattered by that?" she retorted, finally.

He glanced up at her, trying to contain his frustration. "Look, Laura," he said. "You said yourself you don't want to own me, right?"

He watched her jaw work for a second, but she quickly grumbled, "Right."

"And you don't want commitment. Still right?"

Her features set, she gave him a jerky nod.

His exasperation growing, he asked, "So, where do you get off calling Arlene and Fenella bimbos just because the three of us played a little between the sheets—"

"Spare me the graphic details," she spat out, her voice cracking.

"What the hell do you want from me?" he demanded under his breath.

"I want nothing from you," she flared. "But, I have to give you credit. For a few minutes you really had me going with that love-at-first-sight line. I was starting to feel kind of bad about using *you!* Big laugh on me, don't you think?" she retorted flatly.

Anger flooded through him, and he was hard-pressed not to roar like a wounded lion. Struggling to maintain his outward nonchalance, he treated her to a grin. Inside, he was a raging, bloodied beast.

"Since you're such a great liar, does this mean you don't really believe in leprechauns, either?" she demanded.

He shrugged. "My mother used to say the little people could make even the most ridiculous ideas seem logical."

She frowned. "I gather you're saying the idea of falling in love with me at first sight was ridiculous, but the playful little leprechauns made it *seem* logical? At least long enough for you to get me in the sack? That's charming."

He managed to twist his lips into another false smile. "The leprechauns and I—we're charming guys." Looping his thumb into the neck of his crewneck sweater, he tugged on a chain to show her the silver figure that dangled from it. "See this?" he asked.

She raised her chin, eyeing him suspiciously. "What is it?"

"Look at it, dammit," he growled before he could contain his fury.

After a moment while their eyes and wills warred, her curiosity apparently won out, for she scanned the silver piece he was holding out for her to see.

"I've noticed it before, but I was a little...busy." She cleared her throat, but he could tell she was thinking of exactly when the thing had dangled between her breasts, and what sexy, husky words she was crying out at the time. "Uh—um—it looks like a little grinning leprechaun," she ventured, then her afflicted gaze returned to his face. "So what?"

"So...you asked me if I believed in leprechauns. I've worn this Laughing Leprechaun since my mother gave it to me when I was five," he said quietly. "I think you could say, I believe."

She glared at him. "Okay. I believe you believe in leprechauns. Now, would you mind telling me the whole truth about how you feel about me, for once? Would you call me just another one of your bimbos?"

"Would you prefer that I call you my fiancée?"

She stiffened visibly. He wasn't surprised, though he wasn't pleased either. "Of course not," she blurted, sounding horrified.

Her tone incensed him, but he mastered his impulse to swear. "Okay, baby," he murmured with a bogus flash of teeth. "Then I guess, if Arlene and Fenella are my playtime bimbos, then it would follow that you'd have to be one, too. Happy now?"

He watched, powerless, as naked hurt shimmered in her eyes, and he felt like a rotten, lousy son of a bitch. *Dammit!* Doing this her way was going to be hell on both of them.

10

"OGAN'S HERE," Devlin said. "He's giving us a ride back to the car."

Laura stared blankly at him. "What?" she asked, surreptitiously wiping at a foolish tear. What did she care what he thought? She'd gotten into this affair with the sole idea of having a little fun, so why did it bother her that he had, too?

"I said Ogan's at the door, ready to take us back to the car," Devlin repeated, as he stood. "I imagine they have it unstuck by now. So, where do we go from here?"

She got up, barely aware of what she was doing. "We?" she echoed, startled that she was even considering such an absurd notion after his escapade last night with two local women, and what he'd just admitted to her. "You think we're still going to have anything to do with each other, now?"

He took her arm, and with a chuckle he said, "Laura, if you think I'm going anywhere without you, you're sadly mistaken. I've come this far, and I intend to stay until you find your Irish orphan. So don't bother trying to change my mind."

"What if I insist?"

He laughed, drawing the attention of several other guests. "Since when has that made any difference?"

She moaned with exasperation. "Oh, Devlin, I don't know. I'm not sure I can handle being around while you're—you're—pulling your sexual stunts with half the women in the country."

"Why not?"

Unable to believe he'd even asked the question, she stared. "Why not! Why—why—because it's kinky and it's embarrassing to—to have to listen to."

"Oh?" He slanted her a wicked grin. "You listened?"

She flushed. "Not on purpose! But that's not the point. I'm kind of conservative, I guess, and I don't intend to sleep with a man one night and then listen to him satisfy half the town the next. I'm just not put together that way," she insisted morosely. "Call me unenlightened if you must, but I won't have it. If you want to go along with me, no more sex orgies. Is that understood?"

He lifted a brow in what appeared to be amusement. "What about orgies between you and me?"

She felt a rush of unruly desire at his sensual tone. "I think it would be better if we kept our relationship on a purely platonic level from now on."

"That's what you think, huh?" he queried. Indicating the door, he added, "Ogan's waiting. We'd better go."

She didn't care if Ogan was doing the backstroke in clam chowder. She didn't intend to drop this subject until Devlin understood she wasn't kidding. "Devlin," she insisted, drawing his attention. "I'm serious."

The grin he flashed was Machiavellian. "Tell you what, Laura. I won't invite any more ladies to my room late at night. And I'll keep myself completely at your disposal. Use me as long and as thoroughly as you like, then drop me. How's that for a no-strings deal?"

"Don't be silly," she admonished, but she could already feel a shivery excitement at the idea. He was so darned appealing as he stood there smiling at her, his scent doing illicit things to her good sense. "Absolutely not," she forced herself to say, though her teeth were clenched and her tone pitifully unconvincing.

"I promise not to touch you if you don't ask me to." His crooked grin never dimmed, and Laura had the worrisome feeling he fully *expected* her to ask—no, more like *plead!* The egomaniacal pain in the neck!

She turned away, hoping she was wrong, that she would be as strong tonight as her convictions were at this moment. Inadvertently she noticed Ogan, and lamented under her breath, "Oh, dear. I was hoping I'd never have to see that grinning ape again."

"He's a good kid, Laura," Devlin assured her as he gave the young man a friendly wave and spoke in Gaelic to him.

"Oh, no, you don't," Laura protested. "I know he can speak English, so don't pull that stuff on me, today. I don't intend to be left out of the conversation anymore. I could find myself in an Irish harem or something."

He chuckled. "Doubtful, but under the circumstances I'll admit we owe you the English version, this time."

TWENTY MINUTES LATER, they were in the car heading back toward Galway. "How much did you pay them?" Laura asked, after noticing that Devlin had handed the O'Callaghans a few bills.

"Not that much, but I figured they were due something for the hospitality and digging the car out."

"That's true," she admitted as he shifted gears. "But I should have been the one to pay. I had the wreck."

"A wreck I'll remember fondly," he said, his voice tender. "Forget it."

She felt her cheeks heat with mortification, and turned to stare out the window. She knew he wouldn't listen to arguments about the fact that he was without a job and she was on an expense account, so she decided rather than get into another argument with him, she'd simply send him a check after she got back to Florida.

"So," he began, "Mrs. O'Sullivan found something important at the orphanage?"

Laura shrugged. "I don't know how important it is, but when I called Dingle Bay last night, there was a message that she had something for me. I figured, since we can't do anything more in Killannin we might as well go back and check it out."

"Good idea."

Laura had been stewing about something for quite some time—well, at least through a lot of sleepless hours last night—so she decided to ask. "Devlin," she began, "what did you win?"

"Two hundred and fifty pounds."

She looked over at his profile. The morning breeze had tossed his hair, mussing it pleasantly. Every time she saw him she was startled at how unsettling the experience was, affecting her all too much. "That's about five hundred dollars. Pretty good money," she mused aloud, once she'd turned away and found her voice.

He grunted out a brief laugh. "Why the hell else do you think I was making a fool of myself like that if not for the money?"

"Apparently a majority of the women in town didn't see you as much of a fool, considering you won, and were able to take—" She broke off, but the rest of her unfinished thought—*several of them to your bed*—lingered in the air between them, mocking her.

"And?" he asked after a strained silence.

"You know exactly what 'and'!" she muttered. "Why must you insist on dredging it up every few minutes?"

"You brought up the subject, Laura," he reminded her.

She eyed him with irritation, but knew he was right. "Well, I won't anymore."

"Fine with me."

"Just why did you lose your job, anyway?"

He didn't immediately respond, and Laura found herself glancing his way. That wonderfully masculine profile was now forbidding and stern. "Devlin?" she prompted, realizing she'd hit on a very sore nerve.

She'd been upset and wanted to irritate him, but by the rigid set of his shoulders and the white-knuckled way he clutched the steering wheel, she knew she'd gone too far. "Devlin," she repeated tightly. "I'm sorry. I was just kidding."

He growled out a low, ugly oath.

She touched his shoulder, unable to keep from trying to make amends. "Would it help to talk about it?"

He grinned, but the expression was more like a sneer of self-contempt. "If it would help to talk about it, Laura, I'd be a jabbering bore."

"You never know," she urged. "Why don't you try? This thing, whatever it is, has been gnawing at you for a long time."

"On the other hand," he countered, his tone severe, "why don't you talk about your fear and loathing of commitment?"

She felt the sting of his sarcasm. "For your information, I have no fear of commitment."

"Ha," he scoffed. "Little Laura's nose is growing."

She jerked her face away and stared out the window at nothing in particular. The day had grown dark and cloudy, mirroring her mood. "I tell you, I'm not afraid of commitment. It's—it's the *lack* of commitment I've run into that scares the life out of me."

"Dammit," he grumbled. "What the hell was wrong with the men you've hooked up with?"

"Not much. They just had this fantasy about how life was supposed to be, and when it didn't turn out the way they thought it should, they left." She crushed her hands together. "Sort of like your perfect-family fantasy. I keep telling you there is no such thing."

"Like hell," he said.

"Okay, fine," she allowed tiredly. "Live in your fantasy world and talk to your fantasy little people. Just don't expect me to play pretend with you, Devlin, because I refuse to do it anymore."

"I don't expect you to do one damned thing for me, Laura," he countered grimly. "If you'll recall, our deal was I do whatever you ask for as long as you ask. Period."

"What if I ask you to take a flying leap?" she muttered.

"I thought you weren't into kink," he returned, his tone goading. "But if you insist, we can give it a try tonight."

She threw him a grimace that would have disabled lesser men. "I presume you've had loads of practice already today, with the O'Jezebel twins?"

He chuckled, sounding almost amused. "That wouldn't be jealousy in your voice, would it?"

To her annoyance, she found herself starting to blush. "Ha! I scoff at the very idea!" It was a lie, unfortunately. She *was* jealous—she was green and crawly with the stuff—but she continued on. "You can just dangle from all the chandeliers in Europe with all the busty blondes you like, and I'll be completely—completely—blasé!" That word was becoming very useful on this trip, she noticed.

Giving him a thin, cantankerous smile, she snapped, "If you want to know the truth, I don't believe you were really having all that much sex, anyway!" She clamped her mouth shut. What had she said? She didn't believe they'd had all that much sex? Where had that idea come from? Wishful thinking? Were the depraved leprechauns playing tricks with her lips? Had she stumbled into Foot-in-Mouth Hell? Why in the world must she keep harping on a subject that disturbed her so? Would her perverse absorption with this man and his sexual appetites not be satisfied until she had a blow-by-blow—she cringed at the word choice—of the sordid sexy details of this morning's giggly Gaelic group grope?

Wishing she were dead, she sat stunned, unable to take her eyes away from Devlin's profile. Apparently her subconscious had been working overtime in an attempt to get her to further humiliate herself in front of this man.

When he shifted her way, she caught her breath. A wayward quirk played at one corner of his expressive mouth. "What makes you think we didn't have kinky sex this morning?" he queried.

He was provoking her, she knew. He was ready, willing and able to prove to her that he and his two snickering companions— That was it! Two *snickering* companions! She knew what had been bothering her, now. It had been in the back of her mind all along, but she'd just managed to figure it out this minute. Sitting forward, determined and renewed in her conviction, she said, "They were laughing too much, Devlin. *That's* why!"

His grin grew wider, dazzling white against his tanned skin. "You're grasping at straws. Sex can be fun."

She scowled at him. "But after a while the laughter gives way to—to sighs, then panting, then . . ."

He'd had to turn back to watch the road, but still grinning he offered, "Gives way to what? Howling, maybe?"

An unwelcome blush crept up her cheeks at the reminder of exactly what she'd yearned for last night, but never experienced. She reeled to glare out the window. Green fields sped by, pretty as a picture, and a movie-set-perfect village lay in a valley before them, but Laura wasn't in the mood for sightseeing. "I wouldn't know," she ground out.

There was a palpitating silence, but for the rumbling croon of the car tires against pavement. Laura's heart beat so loudly she found herself counting the heavy, rapid beats that pounded in her ears. She had no idea how much time passed, but after a while, Devlin startled her out of her nerve-racked despondency by saying, "You'll find out, Laura. I promise."

Her face stiff with animosity, she snapped, "Find out what?"

"What it's like to howl, *acushla*. Tonight."

She was horrified at how happy that soft pledge made her. Fighting it, she warned, "Don't count on it."

He'd turned back to watch the road. His only response was the slight pursing of his lips.

"And what does that *ack—use—la* thing mean?" she asked, irritated that he was so casual and sure of himself.

"I'll tell you what it doesn't mean," his tone low. "It doesn't mean bimbo."

She frowned in confusion. Was that supposed to be a compliment or was he baiting her again? Crossing her arms before her with a shrug, she muttered, "Be still, my heart."

"And you're right."

When he didn't go on, she glowered at him, knowing he was using her curiosity to get her to respond. "What am I right about?" she asked warily.

"Arlene and Fenella and I didn't have sex."

Her anger eased and confusion took its place. "Sure. They were up there discussing politics with you at five in the morning."

He smiled. "You have to admit, sometimes politics can be pretty comical."

She rolled her eyes heavenward. "Give me a break, Devlin."

"I was teaching them to play poker."

She looked at him askance. "Are you on some sort of medication I should know about?"

He laughed, and she found herself studying his sexy mouth, her irritation muted by the sensuality of his pleasantly curved lips.

"I was teaching them to play poker," he repeated. "Between the Sheets, to be exact."

"Did I ask you for your whereabouts?" she protested. "Poker, my foot!"

"Would you like me to teach you?"

"Don't bother," she muttered grudgingly. "I've graduated from your course."

"Poker, Laura," he said again. "It's a card game."

"I've heard of poker," she retorted. "And I've heard of stupid alibis, too, but poker at five in the morning? That's the stupidest one I've ever heard." Feeling a strange buoyancy, a crazy new hope that he was telling the truth, she added, "I've played poker once or twice, Devlin. It wasn't all that funny."

"You've never played poker with *me*," he insisted softly.

There was perfectly vile devilment in his gaze. She wanted to believe him so badly, she hoped she wasn't going off half-cocked, here. "Really?" she asked at last. "You were really playing poker?"

He nodded. "Jealous?"

She bristled. "Quit asking me that. I told you no!"

He shrugged and turned back to watch the road.

After a time spent stewing and agonizing, she snapped around to face him. "Just why were you teaching two women to play poker at five in the morning?"

He said nothing while he maneuvered the car into a parking spot. Only then did he turn to her, and with an oddly crafty expression, said, "That's my business, Laura. No strings, remember?" Indicating the direction with a nod, he added, "We're here."

She glanced past him, without a bit of interest in rummaging in another dusty old box of dusty old clothes, but she realized she needed to do her job. Her pique simmering, she fumbled for the car door. "Okay. Let's go," she muttered.

When she'd scrambled from the car, scurried up the steps and gone inside, she came crashing to a halt and sniffed the air in the hallway. Before she could be sure what was bothering her, Devlin had reached her side.

She turned to him, and noting his uneasy expression, she grew alarmed. He, too, was also aware that something was very wrong. "Oh, my Lord," Laura whispered. "Do you smell it?"

Devlin nodded, and they both glanced around. "I see it!" She pointed toward the second-floor landing where smoke was starting to billow, but Devlin was already sprinting up the staircase. She dashed after him, crying, "Oh my Lord! *Fire!*"

HOURS LATER, THEY WERE slumped tiredly in the car. Devlin smiled over at Laura. "You look awful," he kidded.

She smiled as she leaned back and closed her eyes. She was startled at how lighthearted she felt, considering the day they'd spent, first rounding up children and getting them to safety across the street. Then, after the fire brigade got the blaze contained, she and Devlin had spent long, tiresome hours moving smoke-blackened possessions from the damaged living quarters into classrooms or storerooms, anywhere there was space. Now, as dusk was falling, they both looked like they'd been showering under a volcanic eruption. They were soot-blackened, and Laura could feel grit everywhere—behind her eyelids, between her teeth—and it glared back at her from beneath her ruined fingernails.

The kids were all fine, thank heavens. Actually, from all the laughter she'd heard, it had sounded as though the children felt like they'd been on an adventure rather than involved in a near tragedy. Laura sighed aloud. "What a day."

"You were something else," Devlin told her. "Remind me never to get on your bad side. I saw you single-handedly carry out a kid under one arm and a four-drawer dresser under the other."

She opened her eyes and winced at the gravelly feel. "That's not true at all. You must have been driven insane by the smoke."

He chuckled, and the wonderful, deep sound of it thrilled her more than she cared to admit. He'd been the amazing one, working tirelessly, carrying children from the hospital ward. She'd seen him with a child in each arm—a sickly boy and a girl with a broken leg. He'd moved them swiftly, yet gently, so as not to injure them further. She marveled at his quick thinking in the emergency. Why, if he hadn't been there to aid poor hysterical Mrs. O'Sullivan, Laura didn't know what sort of catastrophe this whole thing might have become.

"Ready for a shower and a meal?" he asked, interrupting her thoughts.

She nodded, leaning back and exhaling with exhaustion. "I'm starving and filthy. Bath first."

"Check. By the way, what happened to that box of Maureen's they were going to give us?"

Laura didn't even open her eyes as he moved the car out into traffic. "Mrs. O'Sullivan was so upset, I didn't have the heart to bother her about it. I figure if we go back first thing in the morning, we can catch her before she gets too busy."

"Sounds good. Meanwhile, how about staying in the same place as last time we were here?"

"Fine. As long as it has hot, running water and food."

"And a bed?" he asked.

She felt a quiver. It had been an innocent-enough query, so why the overreaction? She supposed it was their recent past, and its association with a bed, that made her heart rate soar. "I could sleep on a pile of broken glass tonight," she said, manufacturing a yawn in hopes he wouldn't detect her nervousness.

"I'll ask for a bed, anyway," he answered, almost too quietly for her to hear.

She opened her eyes a fraction. "Maybe you ought to get two rooms, Devlin." When he passed her a lazily seductive grin that told her he had no such plans, she swallowed, terribly confused about what to do. He wanted her, that was obvious. And she wanted him. That was a shame. Adding to her troubles, he'd been so darned exciting and heroic this afternoon, calming Mrs. O'Sullivan and directing rescue operations until the fire brigade had arrived to take over the job, that she loved him just a little for that alone! Plus the fact that he'd convinced her he actually had only played poker with Arlene and Fenella that morning. She couldn't believe she was really swallowing that weird story, but she was.

In her heart, she knew she shouldn't allow Devlin to touch her again, to love her in all the hot, sexy ways he could. But she was aching for him to do just that, even though she was filthy and her muscles throbbed with stress and strain. She could think of nothing but the feel of his hands on her body, lifting her to the brink of ecstasy, and then, with utterly gentle expertise, catapulting her into divine oblivion. *Oh, Devlin, Devlin, Devlin. What to do, what to do . . .*

The next thing she knew, a hand was holding hers. "Laura? Wake up. We're here."

She stirred, her lashes fluttering open when she realized that she'd fallen asleep. Devlin's face was close above her as he leaned in on her side of the car. She smiled up at him and touched his smudged face. "You're a mess," she murmured sleepily. The charming devil-try in his grin drew her like a moth to flame, and in her dreamy stupor, she was too off her guard to try to re-sist.

He covered the hand on his cheek and slid it to his lips, kissing her palm. "I'm afraid you're going to have to share a room with this mess. They only had one left. A festival's in town."

She laughed, unsure why. The last thing in the world she should do was share a room with Devlin Rafferty. "Another festival?" she asked, her tone skeptical. "What festival, this time?"

With a grin, he tugged her from the car. "Does it matter?"

"It could. If it concerns picking Galway's most prime bachelor."

"It's more like picking Galway's most prime goat," he said, tucking her fingers securely within his and aiming her toward the door.

"That's my favorite kind of festival," she kidded. "Let's go."

"You'll be busy," he warned, his voice low and meaningful.

She stared at his handsome, soot-streaked profile, unable to conjure up any desire to object. Some basic female instinct in her knew he was right. Tonight she would be busy. Tonight he would take her to sexual places she had never been—and she would finally, blissfully, howl.

Without comment, and putting aside all rational objections, Laura allowed him to lead her toward that promised destiny. She even found herself trembling with heady anticipation—fool that she was.

11

DEVLIN WAS A PERFECT gentleman. He left Laura to her privacy as she bathed in their room's huge old claw-footed tub, soaking away the grime of the day. She knew he must be as tired and grimy as she, but he'd gone to sit on their small balcony, his feet propped on the iron railing, to silently watch the sun go down. He'd made no demands on her at all—well, except possibly for the teeny tug on her heart caused by his sensitivity and thoughtfulness.

An hour later, Laura sat at a tiny table in one of the hotel's dining areas, warmed by a blazing turf fire as she munched on cod-roe pâté and wheat crackers. As she waited for Devlin to join her after his shower, she found herself able to think of little else but him—how hero-ically he'd behaved this afternoon, how gallantly he'd behaved this evening. And how tenderly he made love— *Darn*. Why did she insist on dredging up mem-ories of the two of them entwined and writhing in pleasure? Was she falling for the guy? Was she that much of an idiot—even after all the lectures she'd given herself over the years?

The room where she sat was lit only by candlelight and the earthy-scented flames in the hearth. She in-haled the pungent odor and took another bite of pâté. Life was odd, she mused. Very odd indeed. Next month at this time, she'd be in Florida in her cramped, win-dowless office, probably double-checking a list to be published in area newspapers with hundreds of bank-account holders with accounts that had been inactive for more than five years. It was the law that these names be publicized periodically, and it was a satisfying thing to have many of these people reunited with their money. But, "satisfying" was a relative term she was discovering. She knew now that nothing in her life would ever quite measure up again, she feared, to today.

She had no doubt that somewhere—probably in the vast middle of that bank-account list—she would recall this day, this peat fire, even this pâté and the man who would soon share them with her. It would be like recalling a dream, a precious dream. And she would feel a poignant tug on her heart over the sad fact that such illusive dreams couldn't last.

Something touched her cheek, and she realized she was being kissed. She turned and was startled to find inviting, warm lips pressed against hers. She recognized those lips, so strong, yet persuasively gentle, and even though she knew they were being watched, she didn't draw away. She planned on making her dream as memorable as she could, for all too soon she would have nothing left of it but soft memories—like an Irish mist, seductive and haunting, but impossible to possess.

His kiss was very light, very courtly, really, but the encounter wreaked havoc with her nervous system. There was buzzing and tingling and all manner of fluttering in her stomach. Silly schoolgirl stuff, but no less lovely on a rainy Irish night.

When he drew away, whispering an endearment that made her blush, she could only smile. The man was so outrageously beautiful, standing there in black wool-gabardine slacks, Kiltie slip-ons, and an upscale jac-

quard sweater with a distinctive white-and-black dia-
mond pattern. Beneath the sweater, he wore a button-
down white shirt, its collar open. She gave him an ap-
praising once-over and said, "You clean up nice."

He laughed as he took his place across from her. "So
do you," he murmured, his regard thoroughly approv-
ing.

She silently disagreed. Her green tunic sweater was
four years old and the black-and-green stretch stirrup
pants had been a fifty-percent-off bargain at a dis-
count-store sale. In her opinion, she looked like a Rag-
gedy-Ann doll compared to the casually elegant man
lounging across from her. Yet, the admiration she saw
in his smile made her feel less conspicuously "sale rack"
than she had in quite some time. She had to give Devlin credit. He could make a woman feel singularly important when he set his mind to it.

She sighed, weary of the days they'd spent sparring.
All she wanted in the world right now was for this evening to be real between them. No evasions, no half-
truths, no sarcasm or baiting. Pinning him with a serious look, she said, "You're planning on seducing me
tonight, aren't you."

He watched her with interest, then a wry smile
tugged at one corner of his mouth. "I won't say the
thought of making love with you tonight hasn't crossed
my mind. But, this is your game, Laura. I'll play by
whatever rules you choose."

"You only booked one room," she reminded him.

"Goats, remember?" he said softly.

Before she could reply, the waitress came and told
them the specialty of the evening: mussels in wine and
cream, vegetables and walnuts and a white-chocolate-
mousse cake for dessert. Not terribly interested in food

at the moment, Laura absently nodded when Devlin suggested it sounded good. She was starving, but with him so close, she knew she would taste nothing. She might as well order wadded newsprint over shredded cardboard—it would all be the same to her.

They sipped black tea, listening to the music of a small Irish band filtering through from the hotel's main dining room. Laura had seen the ensemble as she'd been ushered to the more intimate chamber. There had been five musicians playing one jiggety air after another on a tin whistle, guitar, fiddle, pipe and drum.

As their dinner was served, the band embarked on another tune. This one was low-pitched and plaintive, its melody brimming with loneliness and tears, while the pulsating beat of the lone drum added a primitive sensuality to the piece. The throbbing lament that drifted from the instruments conjured up images that were melancholy, yet impassioned and singularly Gaelic.

"It's so Irish," Laura murmured. "Beautiful and sad."

He nodded, his smile as pensive as the ballad. "'I will arise and go now,'" he recited with the music as a somber backdrop, "'and go to Innisfree, / And a small cabin build there, of clay and wattles made; / Nine bean rows will I have there, a hive for the honey bee, / And live alone in the bee-loud glade....'"

He glanced up at her when he'd finished, and she couldn't help but smile, though he grew indistinct as sentimental tears marred her vision. How ironic that Devlin Rafferty, though American born, seemed the essence, the personification, of the quiet strength that was Ireland. The realization of what a powerful, lasting impression both the country and the man had made on her in such a short period of time, made her shiver.

"What's that quote from?" she asked, managing to keep her voice sounding even.

"Yeats," he said. "There's a charming innocence in those words, don't you think?"

"Yes, I do," she agreed, but not for the reasons he'd meant. She was charmed by the man who'd quoted Yeats—by his flawless brogue, but even more by the vulnerability that glimmered in his eyes. These were the things that touched her most deeply. Though the beauty of Yeats was undeniable, this American expatriate and his tragic glance was infinitely more so.

"Devlin..." she managed finally, when the touching melody had waned away and the band had begun a more familiar tune, "Danny Boy."

He turned toward the fire, looking as though he'd gone far, far away. When he didn't react, she realized he hadn't heard her. Reaching out, she touched his hand, repeating, "Devlin?"

The contact with her fingers brought him back, and he faced her again. She wasn't shocked after all this time with him, to see the pain of his secret sorrow evident in his gaze, though he tried valiantly to mask it with a careless grin. "What?" he asked, then threw in conversationally, "How's your dinner?"

"Devlin," she persisted, taking his fingers in hers. "Please tell me what's been bothering you. For a week now, we've fought with each other, traveled all over Ireland together, had a wreck and—and made love." She hesitated, but recharged her courage with a quick intake of breath. "I want to know what happened that hurt you so much. I *need* to know."

His smile faltered and his expression grew guarded. Shaking his head, he muttered, "I don't—can't talk about it, yet."

She squeezed his hand, whispering, "Devlin, it's time."

He frowned, his expression like that of someone who had been kicked in the gut. "Get off it, Laura," he growled. "There's nothing I can do about it, so why dig it up?"

"Devlin," she objected, "if it didn't help to talk about things, psychiatrists would all be selling shoes in Sears."

"Maybe they'd be performing a more useful service," he muttered.

"Don't be bullheaded," she objected. "Talk to me!"

When he turned to stare at her, her throat tightened. His handsome face was twisted with agony and his broad shoulders heaved as his breathing became labored. "Damn it to Hades, Laura," he snarled, under his breath. "All right. Since you won't let go of this thing, I hope my little soul-purging is entertaining for you. I'd hate to be a bore."

She clutched his fingers harder. "Don't think insults are going to get me mad enough to walk off and save you from doing this. It's time," she whispered sharply. "You need to get this off your chest, or you'll never heal."

His lip curled with self-loathing. "I'll tell you what I need. What I need is the power to bring a mutilated, molested sixteen-year-old girl back to life. That's what I *need*." His features fierce with grief, he demanded, "Can you help me do that? I can see by your face, you're not sure you can. What the hell did you expect was wrong? Something simple and sexual, like being fired for getting the boss's wife pregnant? Some good old wholesome sins of the flesh maybe?"

A sensation of nausea swept over her at the ugly vision his words summoned. "Devlin," she said, her voice bleak. "I don't believe that. How did— How could you be responsible for such a horrible thing?"

She flinched beneath his withering glare. "How?" he sneered. "Why, Laura. Can't you tell? I'm a goddamn genius, that's how," he muttered. "Prince of the Underdog. That's what they called me in the public defender's office. I was champion of the poor, the wrongly accused, who couldn't afford a lawyer. I could read a man and know he was telling the truth. Never wrong. Damn genius." He laughed bitterly, drawing curious looks. "Then, by heaven, I went into that courtroom and through my brilliant oratory got those penniless bastards off. Case closed. Chalk up another victory for blind justice and the Chicago P.D.'s office." He ran a hand through his hair, and Laura noted with wrenching distress that it was shaking badly.

His voice cracking, he rasped, "Devlin Rafferty, recently promoted to Chief Public Defense Lawyer for Chicago, had a perfect record. Never lost a damn case—" He broke off, and with a muttered oath pushed up from the table, growling, "Hell, I can't do this...."

Before Laura had time to object or even jump to her feet, he'd struck out the door, melting into the misty darkness.

She got up, grumbling, "Not this time, Devlin Rafferty. You're not running away from it this time!" Hurrying outside after him, she called, "Devlin? Wait! We have to talk!"

She could hear the click of a man's footsteps, quickly disappearing somewhere off in the distance. "Devlin? I'm not going back until we talk!" she insisted. "I don't know this city. I could get lost and die."

The sound of the footsteps became fainter and fainter.

"Or—or I could get attacked by marauding, festive goats," she tried, but only halfheartedly. She doubted that he could hear her anymore, or that he particularly cared what might happen to her. She'd never seen him so hostile, so broken-up before.

She shivered, hugging herself against the wet chill. "Devlin?" she repeated, but hardly loud enough to be heard a foot away. "Please—don't do this...." With a sigh, she knew it was no use calling after him. But, she wasn't going to let him get off this easily. Running away wouldn't solve anything. Not sure why she was making his private horror her business, she headed down the sidewalk, keeping one hand sliding along the slick stone wall so she wouldn't accidentally fall off an unseen curb and break her leg. She'd be darned if she was going to let him carry this burden around all by himself. He needed a friend, and she planned to be that friend.

She frowned. Friend? Is that what she wanted to be to Devlin? She strained to see into the distance. "Devlin?" she called more loudly. "You're going to have to walk into the sea to get away from me. I'm not giving up, is that clear?"

Silence.

"Don't be a coward, Devlin," she challenged. "Come back and talk to me about it."

She reached a street lamp and hesitated, grasping the metal pole. "I'm still coming, Devlin, but I'm getting disoriented in the fog. There's a curb here. Which way do I go?" Her teeth chattered. "It's—it's cold out here, Devlin. But I'm not going back."

More silence.

Darn your stubborn hide! she admonished, shaking again with the cold.

"'Evenin', missy," came a slightly drunken salutation from behind Laura.

"Why—er—hello...." she said, startled as she stared up into the face of a rather unscrupulous-looking young man with a decided lack of front teeth.

"Yer a mighty fair lass ta be out here shoutin' after some blitherin' coward, y'know." He grasped her arm. "I'd be pleased if ya would go with me, and down a few stouts in MacKenny's Pub."

"I couldn't possibly," she said with a stiff smile. "I'm meeting someone."

He leered at her and swayed, as though he were on board a ship, his grip tightening probably more to keep him upright than for any evil purpose. Laura gulped and tried to pull away. She was unsuccessful.

"Sounds ta me, me girl, like the bloke ain't worth the cost of a wee pint. Come on with ol' Jimmy, here. I'm a tolerable buck, so says me ma, God bless 'er, when she's sober."

"Please," Laura objected, trying again to yank free of his grasp. "I'm waiting for someone."

He cackled, and wiped his nose on his faded wool shirtsleeve. "Some bloody tosser, sounds to me like. Leave him be. If ye fancy a real man, now, *that* I am, y'know."

She was getting angry. The man didn't seem too threatening, just annoying. But enough was enough! "Look," she insisted. "if you don't let go of me, I'm going to kick you so hard between your wobbly legs you'll be a bent-over soprano for a month!"

He frowned and swayed again, this time almost back far enough to fall over. "Now, I ask ya, is that friendly?" he queried. "All I want ta do is buy ya a wee drink."

"I'm counting to three, *Jimmy*, and if you don't let go of me by the time I do, your *manly* days are going to be over for a while," she warned in her most assertive voice. She squinted determinedly at him, trying to imagine this weaving drunk as the store manager who'd once refused to take back her new toaster that, after a week, had begun to fling toaster pastries at the ceiling, where they'd stick until scraped off. The pastries had been unfit for eating, but high entertainment for Sally. Laura had had a rough time with the hawk-nosed jerk of a manager, but she'd stuck to her guns. She'd paid good money for that toaster, and planned to get one that didn't shoot baked goods into orbit. Finally she'd won. And she would again, right now. Lifting her I-will-get-my-money-back chin a notch higher, she began to count. "Okay, fella. Here goes. One... two...th—"

"Bloody hell, woman," he barked, abruptly releasing her. "Have a care about me jewels, now." He backed unsteadily away, grousing, "If I may say, lassie, yer beauty's a waste with that wicked tongue ye have in yer head, y'know." It only took a few halting steps for the drunk to disappear into the mist, but it wasn't until Laura was sure he'd gone that she breathed with relief.

Though she hadn't admitted it to herself until that moment, she'd been a little frightened. The guy was thin, but nearly six feet tall, and probably had a good fifty pounds on her. If he'd really wanted to force her to go with him, she'd have had a hard time stopping him.

She glanced distractedly about. The muted glow of the streetlight didn't provide much illumination in the thick fog. When another teeth-rattling shiver convulsed her body, she drew her arms about herself and rubbed, trying to create friction warmth. It was too cold to continue the search, she realized unhappily. If she didn't plan to catch her death out here, she'd have to go back. What she wouldn't have given for one of those smelly Irish sweaters right now. Heaving a long, disheartened moan, she mumbled, "Devlin, where are you?"

A movement caught her eye, and she stiffened, fearing the drunk had returned. "Devlin. Thank goodness. . . ."

Her happiness at his return diminished as she scanned him with searching disquiet. He'd propped himself against a light post, his hands shoved into his pockets. He looked so very handsome, but so very unhappy. She wanted to comfort him, love him— She bit her lip.

The white in his sweater seemed very white in the murky night, giving his shoulders a breadth that looked almost as wide as the walkway. He stood so still, his expression was sad, yet so gentle as he watched her.

"I—I'm glad you came back," she said through chattering teeth.

He shook his head in what looked like self-reproach. "I guess old habits die hard. I still run to the aid of the underdog."

"You—you heard?"

He shrugged. "Yeah. But by the time I got here, I wasn't sure who needed my help." He lifted a reproachful brow. "Laura, it's not polite to threaten a man's jewels."

Somewhere in there, she'd heard a bit of the teasing, playful Devlin she'd first met. A slow grin blossomed on her face. Without thinking, she went to him and slid her arms about his middle, cuddling close. "Devlin. I'm freezing. Let's go inside—where we can talk. . . ."

She felt him stir, and knew he was removing his hands from his pockets. Soon he was pulling her against him, again, his lips grazing her hair. "*Acushla*," he murmured against her temple. "Can't you leave me alone about this?"

She shook her head, hugging him. "No, I can't." With a kiss on his cheek, she added, "And for the last time, tell me what that word means."

Disengaging himself, he draped an arm about her shoulders and began to guide her back toward the hotel. "It means, 'little bully,'" he whispered.

She eyed him askance. "It does not."

He gave her a brief smile. The expression was small and wayward, but it was *real,* and the sight made her heart soar.

THEIR COZY ROOM WAS warm, illuminated only by a freshly lit fire. The stubby metal head and footboard of the bed were tinted gold to mimic brass, and a quilt in shades of pale blue, yellow and green covered the thick mattress. The worn wooden floor shone with fresh polish, but creaked underfoot, and the wallpaper was a riot of faded blue rosebuds. Still, to Laura, it was the loveliest room she had ever seen—because Devlin was there.

He stood before the stone hearth watching her, not quite scowling, as she perched on the frayed settee that faced the fire, and waited.

She'd retired to the bathroom to change into jeans and a red cotton sweater, and while she was in there, he'd put on his sweats. But even in such basic attire, he was no less elegant—just more inviting. She forced herself to remain staunch in her commitment. She would simply refuse to melt in the face of his male allure. She would wait. He was going to get this thing off his chest if their standoff had to last until they both turned into stone.

"You're not going to back down, are you?" he asked wearily.

She shook her head.

"You're sure you want to hear this?"

"No. But you need to say it. So, I'm going to listen."

"*Hell,*" he groused, but there was a resigned tone to it, as though he'd finally decided she was right. The time had come to talk.

She smiled encouragingly, and patted the settee in invitation.

His assenting exhale was rough as he took a seat. She knew he was still very reluctant. Every muscle in his body appeared tense. Wanting to help, she reached over and touched his hand. He startled her by taking it and holding on.

"So, tell me," she urged.

He looked up at the ceiling, then stared into the fire again. Suddenly, he seemed to have departed, gone back to Chicago to confront whatever it was head-on, for his lips had grown tight and grim.

"His name was Kevin O'Kelly," Devlin began, his voice low and harsh. "A fresh-faced kid. Seventeen, right off a Missouri farm." He grimaced. "O'Kelly. Nice Irish name, don't you think?" he muttered, more to himself than to her. "Seemed like an innocent-enough kid. No record. Scared and confused when Tony brought him in. Swore he'd just gotten off the bus from Poplar Bluff."

Devlin ran both hands through his damp hair as he worked to regain control. "There'd been a kid on the bus, but nobody could be sure it was Kevin, and the cops couldn't prove it wasn't. But, a witness thought she'd seen a blond, blue-eyed teenager at the scene of a rape out behind a Chicago movie theater. Swore it was Kevin. But it had been a dark night. The victim couldn't remember a thing. She'd been traumatized pretty badly. A friend of mine, a cop, was sure the kid had done it. But, no, I believed the kid's story. Me, the genius." His mouth twisted ruefully. "Naturally I *used* the kid's youth and innocent looks, his blue-eyed all-American farm-boy image, and I got him off."

Laura understood, now. She closed her eyes, unable to imagine the torture he'd been going through. "So— so after he got off," she stammered weakly, "he went out and—and killed a girl?"

"Hell, no," Devlin corrected with a malignant laugh. In a lightning-fast motion, he vaulted up, visibly trembling with the violence of his emotions. He thrust himself toward the mantel, clutching it brutally, as his broad shoulders slumped forward in defeat. "No," he repeated in a haggard whisper. "That's not quite right, Laura. After *I* got the slime off, he went out and *raped, tortured and killed* a little kid on her way home from a baby-sitting job. Mary Anne—that was her name— Mary Anne was earning money to go to—to college. Wanted to be a teacher..." His words trailed off in a half sob.

Unable to bear sitting back and watching his agony any longer, she moved closer to him in an instinctive need to comfort. "Devlin," she cried softly, encircling his chest with her arms and nuzzling his stiffened back.

"It wasn't your fault. You couldn't have known what that . . . Kevin would do."

She felt his revulsion at the mention of the murderer's name in his shudder.

"I should have known," he groaned. "I should have seen through his 'aw shucks, sir' country-boy shit. Tony did."

"Has Tony ever been wrong?"

Devlin snorted. "Not according to him."

She slipped beneath his arm and came around to face him, looking up into his face. "But, has he?" she insisted softly.

He eyed her solemnly for a moment. "Sure, he's been wrong."

She lifted her arms to his shoulders. "So, now you've been wrong, too. It happens."

He hesitated, measuring her grimly for a moment. Then, his eyes taking on the same old sheen of self-hatred, he shook his head and cursed. "Mary Anne's still dead."

The anguished statement stabbed her heart. Not knowing how to help, impulsively she stood on tiptoes and kissed his rigid jaw. "Yes, she is, Devlin," Laura admitted unhappily. "But maybe it's time you started trying to put an end to your pain."

He shook his head resolutely. "No. It isn't that easy."

"And running away is better?" she challenged, praying she was doing the right thing.

He scowled, but said nothing for a long time.

"Well?" she coaxed, wanting to know what was going through his mind.

"No," he ground out, finally. "It hasn't been better."

Grateful for his truthfulness, she nodded. "Thank you," she whispered, and then had to ask, "Did they—catch him?"

He swallowed. "Mary Anne . . ." His voice broke at the mention of the dead girl's name. Clearing his throat, he went on, "Mary Anne tore his coat in the struggle, and his wallet fell out. He stole a car, and crashed it into a tree trying to get away from the cops."

Devlin said nothing more for a moment, and Laura could only stand there mutely, a tear of compassion sliding down her cheek, as she observed the wretched play of emotions on his handsome face.

"What happened?" she asked, wiping away the tear.

"Bastard died in the hospital about the time I was turning in my resignation," he said without inflection, as though he were drained, body and soul.

Heartsick at his desolate expression, she released him. And taking one of his hands, still clenched around the stone mantelpiece, she murmured, "Come with me."

He didn't resist, and she wasn't surprised. Letting out all his private suffering had clearly rendered him exhausted both physically and mentally. When they reached the bed, she turned down the covers and ordered softly, "Get in."

He considered her, his expression questioning, but he said nothing.

She smiled faintly at his confusion. "I was just wondering, Devlin . . ." She paused to gather her courage. When she had, her decision was set in stone. She would hold this hurting man tenderly, love him sweetly, or roughly if he preferred—whatever it would take to help him begin to expunge the awful ache of guilt from his heart.

She cared about him. Cared very much. Maybe too much. She would offer whatever gentleness and affection she was capable of giving—and in the most basic, primal way a woman could ease a man's grief.

She would make love to him the way she had made love to no man before. It was strange how very much she wanted this, now. It wasn't just sex anymore, with Devlin. It was more than that. He'd shown himself to be a man of such strength and noble caring—Devlin Rafferty, Prince of the Underdog, savior of fire-ravaged orphans. She liked that about him. Quite possibly, she loved it....

Giving his fingers a meaningful squeeze, she asked him shyly, "Show me what I can do—to make things better."

12

DEVLIN DIDN'T MOVE, only watched her, the disbelief on his face utterly irresistible. To prove that she meant what she'd said, she sat down on the bed and pulled her sweater over her head, tossing it into the shadows. She didn't smile at him, could barely meet his eyes. She was unaccountably bashful, considering the fact that they weren't exactly strangers.

As the firelight turned his eyes to flame, she was suddenly filled with a new, hot desire to have this man love her—deeply, soundly, whether she ever howled or not. Unfastening the waistband of her jeans, she felt like a temptress, and managed a timid grin. "Do you want me, Devlin?" she asked, her voice so hushed, so seductive she was shocked at herself.

His luminous eyes widened slightly at her unexpected tone, and his lips lifted with the beginnings of a crooked smile. "I always have, *Acushla*."

She gave him a furtive look as she slipped out of her jeans. "Are you calling me a little bully again?"

He sat down on the edge of the bed and pulled his sweatshirt off over his head. His eyes glowing with a new heat that had nothing to do with the fire, he stretched out a hand and commanded softly, "Come here."

She licked her lips in nervous anticipation, but managed to retain her smile. "*Acushla*," she repeated in a mockingly accusing tone as though she'd called him a bully, too. Then, very deliberately she leaned toward him, dropping her elbows on the quilt to rest her chin in her hands. "How do you like my Gaelic, Devlin?" she queried.

He grinned then, and for some reason he seemed suddenly pleased. "I love your Gaelic," he murmured, leaning forward to brush a kiss along her naked shoulder.

Laura moved into his arms without a note of fanfare, yet with a wealth of feeling, as though she were returning to a loving, happy home, long missed and mourned.

Devlin held her in his embrace, making no move to love her or to touch her anywhere else. She, too, simply clutched him tightly about his wide chest, savoring their silent communion.

All need to tease, to seduce or to be playful vanished. This unexpected sweetness, this quiet melding was new to Laura and held her in awed reverence. She could feel his heartbeat, could hear his deep breathing. How lovely it all was, how lovely and fulfilling—and stimulating beyond anything she had ever known.

By some sort of mental telepathy, their lips finally met, and their lovemaking began with slow, thoughtful kisses and tentative touches. The remainder of their clothes fell away in heedless abandon as his hands moved over her body, working their exotic magic. His mouth traced a sensual path from her jaw to the rosy peaks of her breasts, where his warm lips lingered, exploring, sending little tremors through her body.

The lovers resisted the rush toward climax, but took their time to stroke, to excite, to give each other pleasure. In this ballet of flesh against flesh, soft breasts tingled against a hair-roughened chest, fragile curves were lovingly juxtaposed to bold ruggedness. Exciting hardness was fitted to sweet softness, inciting blood to pound and senses to whirl and reel. Yet, by some unspoken covenant, Laura and Devlin moved with restrained ardor as hands and lips searched and found pleasure points, and sleek bodies grew fiery and moist on their journey toward ultimate intimacy.

Devlin's knowing fingers slid along the silky contours of her back, her thighs, her stomach and on down, with an almost-worshipful languor, while she, too, traced the delicious masculine contours of his muscular chest, belly and buttocks, causing him to groan.

His lips caressed hers as he whispered a word very softly—too softly to make out, but she knew it was that same Irish word—that "little bully" word, and she smiled. "What does it mean, Devlin," she murmured breathlessly. "Really."

"You know what it means, Laura," he coaxed in a sexy rasp, slipping down along her belly, paying sinful homage to every inch of her with his lips, teeth and tongue. "You've always known...."

At his husky declaration, her heart lurched perilously and a frightened quiver surged through her. Oh, Lord, he was right. She did know. She'd probably always known. "My love..." she whispered, positive that this was what *acushla* meant. *My love.* There should never have been any doubt in her mind, but until this second, she'd been unable to acknowledge the truth of it. That love-at-first-sight thing had never been a line, never been a lie. Devlin loved her; had loved her from the beginning. And she—she had—

"Oh, Devlin... *acushla*..." she cried, hating herself, but unable to fight the fact any longer. She was in love with this man, dammit. Unable to help it, to stop it, she opened herself to him, granting him full, dizzying entry, not only to secret physical places, but into her soul, as well.

Clearly he'd heard her soft affirmation, for he hesitated an instant, as though astounded. Then, in a voice that was both grave and loving, he vowed, "Forever, Laura."

Searching, searing lips found the rich moistness of her core, and the depth and urgency of his kisses made her gasp in delicious agony. She writhed in white-hot gratification. With their fingers resolutely entwined, he gave her the ultimate gift between a man and a woman—pure, erotic release. She cried out with joy, and her body quaked, arching as she sighed his name with a new, undeniable reverence. "Devlin... oh...Devlin. I love you...."

Taking his face between her trembling hands, she drew him back up, and with dreamy resolve, began to shower his handsome features with wanton, coaxing kisses. "Love me, Devlin," she pleaded against his throat, her tongue teasing his lobe, then dipping into his ear. "Make me—make me howl...."

His chuckle was deep and sensual, reverberating through her body. "I did promise, didn't I?" he whispered. With a sigh, he kissed the tip of her nose. "But there is the business of being responsible, first."

He rolled away, and Laura felt momentarily bereft. But he didn't go far. His shaving kit was in a drawer beside the bed, and it was only a few seconds before he was ready above her. Pressing his lips to hers, he caressed her mouth more than kissed it. She drank in the sweetness, relishing the honeyed glow that radiated along her limbs. With a moan of need, she hugged his big body to her, reveling in the heat of this sexy, naked haven. "Devlin," she cried softly. "I can't stand it. Please..."

He looked at her, his eyes soft, then lifted himself, bracing over her on powerful arms. Laura expected an exhilarating, deep plunge, and was startled when he repositioned himself, slightly forward, and instead of settling deep inside her, he began to rub gently.

She blinked, her lips opening in surprise at the unexpected flicker of agreeable sensation. Her stunned glance met heavily-lashed blue eyes that were intense, gauging her closely, as he focused wholly on giving her pleasure. His muscles bulged with the effort of balancing himself in a position that would best enhance her arousal.

As she lay beneath him, speechless, unable to do more than relish this new, heady experience, Devlin flashed her a grin that told her he'd registered her bewilderment and was well pleased by her initial reaction.

Each measured dip and rise sent shivery waves of desire through her, each more potent in effect than the one before. She found herself panting, moaning, her consciousness ebbing toward oblivion, then blazing more keenly than ever.

After a delirious span of time, when she thought she could bear no more of the exquisite pain, she closed her eyes, tossing her head helplessly from side to side, her body wet and flaming as she lay there, accepting in disbelief, the glorious, indecent mastery he was exerting over her with the merest flesh-to-flesh caress.

And then it came—pure and blinding—the deepest, most awesome ecstasy she had ever experienced, sweeping out from her core in a golden wave, the electricity of it scorching her body.

And yet, beyond the flood of sensations, the beauty of release, she heard the strangest sound. It was a low-pitched, protracted note, soulful yet jubilant. With a start, she opened her eyes wide, to stare up at Devlin. His regard was bright with male satisfaction, and she abruptly understood why. That sound—that *howl*—had come from her own passion-constricted throat.

He had kept his promise—and exquisitely. . . .

At that instant, she felt his deep thrust, and found herself soaring to another staggering climax as this amazing, beautiful, wicked man summoned his own release.

THE NEXT MORNING, by the light of day, they made love again. It was even more wonderful than the night before, to see his marvelous body poised above her, his features lovingly taut in his desire to please.

They had to laugh when, upon leaving their room, they chanced to meet the elderly couple who had spent the night in the room next door. The two stared worriedly at Devlin and Laura. It was plain that they had been privy to the wild, passionate noises that had permeated the walls, and had no doubt visualized bizarre, deviant behavior going on.

Devlin winked and grinned as if to say the couple's darkest suspicions were absolutely justified. Laura could only blush and tug him along the hallway, hurrying away as the twosome continued to stare with a disapproving glower.

The joy in her soul died on their drive to the foundling home, when Devlin mentioned marriage. Her heart froze, and her throat closed in fear: Why hadn't she told him about Sally? Why hadn't she blurted it out the instant they'd met—in the customs line? No, that would have been silly. Maybe at dinner that first night? But what would have been the reason then? She wasn't the type to bandy about her private business, and never would have considered such a thing.

Maybe she should have told him that first time they'd made love in the loft. But no. This thing between them had only been a small affair then. At least, that's what she'd tried to make it in her mind.

And now? What did she do, now? Now that she knew she was in love with him, and he was talking about marriage? Now that he was looking at her with such devotion? She felt a guilty tremor dart through her every time she met his gaze.

Laura knew it was much too late to be telling this man who doted on the idea of "the perfect family" that he was talking about marriage to a woman with a flawed child. Damn! How could she have been so naive to allow herself to drift so long in this crazy fantasy world, believing that their fling wouldn't touch all areas of her life? Didn't she realize that reality would ultimately have to win out—for better or for worse?

She cringed at unwittingly choosing words universally used in the marriage ceremony; the very words, or rather, the very *promise* Vincent had broken when he walked out on Laura and their retarded baby daughter. As for Matt, even with all his good intentions, he hadn't been able to make it all the way to the altar. He may have been the most deceitful, after all, for he'd managed a nice, six-month affair with Laura before he'd slithered off into oblivion, leaving her and her confused, hurt little girl with nothing but a mumbled apology.

Laura peered over at Devlin, who, seeming to sense her perusal, reached out and caressed her leg, remarking, "You've gone so quiet. Why so serious all of a sudden?"

She smiled faintly, wishing she didn't love the feel of his long fingers splayed intimately along her thigh. "Devlin," she began. "I—I have to explain something."

He removed his hand to downshift as he turned. "Okay," he said quietly. "But we're here." Pulling into a parking space, he looked over at her. "What's on your mind?"

The love in his eyes made a lump form in her throat, and she found she could only shake her head in answer. The vivid memory of Vincent's eyes invaded her mind—she remembered again how his regard had mutated from devotion to disgust at the thought of being saddled forever with an impaired child. And Matt had reacted so similarly, it was startling. He'd gone from spouting his staunch declaration of undying love and commitment to sneaking off in sniveling cowardice.

Laura simply wasn't sure she had the strength to watch Devlin's loving glance go leaden with abhorrence. Of course, there was always that spark of hope that he would be different. Stronger. Gulping hard, she prayed that he was. She so desperately wanted to share everything with him—all the joys and sorrows of life—forever. But that "perfect family" mantra of his kept echoing in her brain, filling her with cruel doubt. "Later," she muttered, opening the door and jumping out, hating her weakness. She knew she had to act like a mature adult. It wasn't fair to Devlin to keep him in the dark, especially now. But she couldn't shake the

nagging dread that her reality would fly too squarely
in the face of Devlin's ideal, and destroy his love for her.

IT WAS A ROWDY PLACE they walked into, but a cheerful
one. Inside the foundling home, the cleanup had begun in earnest, with the older children washing walls
and woodwork, and younger ones carting out smoke-
blackened debris.

Mrs. O'Sullivan ushered them into her office, beaming at Devlin and fawning embarrassingly, her admiration obvious because of his heroic efforts yesterday.
But before Laura could ask about the new information
about Maureen, she was stunned into speechlessness by
a tiny girl curled up on the velvet settee, obviously
confused and frightened. Laura's heart went out to the
child, for she reminded her of her own Sally. The child,
about five years old, also had Down's syndrome.

"Who's this?" she asked, drawing both Mrs. O'Sullivan's and Devlin's attention.

"Ah, 'tis a real shame," Mrs. O'Sullivan lamented
with a shake of her head. "The poor babe is a castoff,
rescued just this day by the local constabulary. 'Twas
an innocent pawn in a confidence game. Lord bless us
all, the lass was forced ta beg in the streets for coins. 'Tis
a crime that happens hereabouts all too often. A hor-
rid shame."

Laura knelt beside the child and smiled at her.
"Hello," she offered, holding out a hand. "How are
you?"

The girl, her almond-shaped eyes glistening with
tears of bewilderment and fear, tentatively put out a
grimy hand, but remained mute.

"*Hell*," Devlin muttered, and the tiny child jumped,
retreating into an even smaller, more frightened ball as

she spied the big, frowning man not far away. "This turns my stomach," he muttered, stalking out of the office.

Laura, who had shifted around to look at him, wasn't quite sure she'd registered correctly what had happened. She felt dazed. This mental haziness was, she realized, a safety device—a self-protective numbing.

"What a shame," Mrs. O'Sullivan remarked in a sad whisper. "Such a grand man, he is. 'Tis a shame this wee human's affliction sickens him so. Yet, I've borne witness to such a sorry thing many's a time in me calling, more's the pity."

Laura came out of her stupor, at least in part, and faced Mrs. O'Sullivan. Though her wits were still oppressively slow, she'd heard what the woman said, and understood what she meant. Devlin was disgusted by the sight of the retarded child. She shuddered violently when the ugly truth penetrated.

The older woman looked away from the door and down at Laura, her expression going from saddened to concerned. "Bless me, child. Is that a wee tear in yer eye?"

An acute sense of loss engulfing her, Laura stood, blinking back the evidence of her deep hurt. The thing she'd feared most in the world was true. In one brutal sentence, and a single glimpse of a handsome face puckered in distaste, she'd learned all that she'd dreaded she would learn. Though she loved Devlin, and knew a part of her always would, she couldn't love his unsympathetic heart.

There was nothing left for her to know—now. Nothing to hope for—now. The horrible suspense was over, and she was drained, body and soul. She couldn't say the outcome was much of a surprise. A crushing calamity, yes, but no surprise.

"Child?" Mrs. O'Sullivan prodded. "Ye look faint. Can I be of help?"

Laura tried desperately to snap herself out of her despair. She had a job to do. After all, it wasn't as though this was the first time a man had failed her horribly. "I'm fine," she assured Mrs. O'Sullivan, though her voice was feeble. With a hard-won professional smile, she asked, "Didn't you have something for me concerning Maureen Renny?"

"Ah, yes." The woman turned to rummage in her desk, and drew out a slip of paper. This surprised Laura, for she'd expected another box of belongings.

"'Twas after ye left I found an old file. Maureen filled out the paper before she was hired, years ago. 'Tis a bit of the luck of the leprechauns that I stumbled on it at all, it is." She smiled kindly, though looking concerned. "There was an abode number scratched on the page, for a Renny in Claregalway." She handed the paper to Laura, adding, "Could be her people reside there yet. The village is but a short drive east."

Numbly Laura nodded.

"Did ye have luck with the sister in Killannin?" Mrs. O'Sullivan asked.

With a shake of her head, she said, "Wasn't in town. If nothing comes of this, I'll call her tonight."

"Ah, 'tis a real shame." Walking around her desk, the foundling-home manager picked up the cowering child, soothing her in a crooning singsong voice. Touching Laura's arm, she offered in the same gentle tone, "Don't fret, lass. Himself, Mr. Rafferty, is a fine man...fer the most part."

Laura managed a weak smile. "I know." Then, facing Mrs. O'Sullivan, she asked, "Would it be possible for me to catch a bus to Claregalway?"

The woman frowned. "Sure, now. But why, when yer man has a grand car?"

Laura couldn't resist the urge to touch the child's wispy blond hair with a finger. "It's—it's just that I—I need to think. Alone . . ."

Mrs. O'Sullivan watched Laura for a moment, then nodded solemnly. "I'll ring up Paddy. He'll give ya a lift." Hiking the little girl onto her other hip, she asked, "What would ya have me tell yer man, then?"

Laura peered out the open window. Devlin was leaning against the hood of the car, but she couldn't see his expression. Did it really matter anymore what he thought—who he loved or didn't love? "Tell him . . ." Feeling a rush of despair at her attempt to put it in words, she couldn't trust her voice, so she shook her head.

"I'll tell him to wait, then," Mrs. O'Sullivan said, picking up the phone and dialing. "Sure, and why don't you go on down the back stairs? Me Paddy, he'll be there directly."

"Thank you," Laura mumbled, unable to meet the woman's pitying scrutiny.

"Not a'tal, a'tal." As Laura started for the door, Mrs. O'Sullivan called after her, "Buck up, lass. No man's perfect."

If she hadn't been so broken up inside, Laura could almost have laughed at that. It was *so* true. No man was perfect. And *dammit*, no woman or child was perfect, either! Sally wasn't, of course, but she had a thousand fine qualities. There was so much about her to love that anyone who got to know her would be crazy about her.

People were human, and all humans were imperfect in one way or another. Devlin, for instance, was intolerant of things he didn't understand. That was his imperfection. Tragically for Laura, intolerance was the one imperfection she simply couldn't forgive.

As she and jolly Paddy O'Sullivan chugged off in the foundling home's rattletrap automobile, she smiled bravely, struggling to be conversational. But her heart wasn't in it. Her entire being was filled with relentless, hopeless doom—no matter what good news she might glean today at the address in Claregalway. Tonight, with Devlin, would be the most wretched, most barren night of her life, for she would have to tell the man she desperately loved—*goodbye.*

13

DARKNESS HAD FALLEN when Laura and Paddy returned from Claregalway. Mrs. O'Sullivan explained that Devlin had stayed all day, pitching in with the cleanup, but when the children had been tucked into their beds, he'd returned to the hotel.

Now, as Laura stared at the door that separated her from the man she loved, she felt battered, sick at heart, her emotions in shreds. In her hand, she clutched a small packet—the answer to her questions about Maureen Renny and the poor orphan child who was about to come into a fortune. It was the absolute proof she'd come in search of. Her job in Ireland was done. Success was hers, yet she was terribly unhappy.

She was seized with anxiety at the thought of what she was about to do to Devlin, to his life. He'd come to Ireland to find peace after a shattering experience, and now she was going to have to destroy whatever peace he might, at the moment, falsely believe he'd found.

Her tears had been bottled up for so many hours her chest felt as if it would explode. She was frightened that at the first glimpse of Devlin, she'd burst into a fit of hysterics.

Somehow, she must find the strength to get through this. She must not let the brutality of the damage she was going to do sway her to take him into her arms, comfort him, love him. Whatever they'd had was over, and she had to remain resolute, for Sally's sake.

Overwhelmed by dread, she turned the doorknob, knowing what she had to do, and sure that it would be the death of something that had seemed so fine and pure—until it had been proved impossible.

When the door creaked open, Laura drew in a breath at the sight of his imposing silhouette, all lean muscle, clad only in sweatpants, his chest and wide shoulders haloed by firelight as he bent to lay aside a book. The Laughing Leprechaun swayed into her view, silver glinting red in the fire's glow. "Laura," he murmured, his voice almost reverent, yet faintly questioning. "What made you decide to go off alone? Mrs. O'Sullivan acted as though she was sworn to secrecy about where you were."

As he rounded the settee, she took an unconscious step backward, flattening herself against the closed door. An urge to run blindly into the night coursed through her, but she knew she had to get this thing finished, so she could try to get on with her life. She forced a pleasant expression. The situation was going to be bad enough without the added pain of angry recriminations.

Before she could react, he was holding her in his arms. In the space of a heartbeat, his lips were hungry and hot against hers. She went rigid at first, but all too quickly found herself accepting his lovemaking with more relish and urgency than her plans allowed.

As firmly as she could, she pulled away, imploring faintly, "Devlin, we have to talk. Please . . . sit down."

Not quite relinquishing his hold, he scanned her face, his features loving, earnest. "I missed you today," he said, brushing her temple with another light kiss that sent a ripple of soul-rending agony through her.

Fighting tears, she insisted, "Please, Devlin." Indicating the settee with a trembling hand, she said, "Let's sit."

He nodded, his face registering a new wariness. "Okay." He took her fingers in his and led her to the seat before the flickering fire. He sat down, pulling her into his lap. "Let's talk," he teased, but his half smile was inquiring, as though he sensed something wasn't quite right.

Within the sexy haven of his lap, she could feel his arousal, and knew he was willing and ready to give her dizzying satisfaction. That knowledge made her shudder with regret. "Devlin—" Her voice wavering, she cleared her throat. "Not now. We have to *talk*." Wriggling from his lap, she perched on the raised stones of the outer hearth, clutching the small package to her chest.

He regarded her silently for a moment, then asked the dreaded question. "What is it, Laura?" His voice and his expression were calm, though guarded.

She swallowed hard, trying to form the most difficult answer of her life. "First," she managed, knowing she was a coward to do it this way, but unable to find the strength to blurt it out. "I want to tell you a story."

He lifted one brow, as though he were dubious, but nodded encouragingly.

"Well," she began, not quite able to meet his questioning gaze. "Once there was this housemaid at Dingle Bay Country House who met a nice couple visiting there on vacation. The young wife and the maid were within five years of being the same age, and because they had things in common, they became friends. After the couple went home, the wife and the maid exchanged letters on occasion. About a year later, the maid wrote to tell the young wife that she was pregnant, and that the baby's father, already married and living in America, would have nothing to do with her."

Laura chanced a peek at Devlin's face. He was watching her with narrowed eyes, but she couldn't tell what he might be thinking.

"Go on," he urged.

She nodded, resigned. "Anyway, the couple invited the maid to come to their town, paying her way. Once there, they put her up in an apartment. You see, in the meantime the wife had learned she couldn't have children, and because the husband was . . . well, older, and had a problem or two with his health, they couldn't adopt. Still, they wanted a child badly, so with the best of intentions, they concocted a not-quite-legal plan to save the young Catholic maid from disgrace, and also gain for themselves the baby they could never have on their own."

Devlin had pursed his lips and was staring into the fire as she continued, "The wife began to pad herself, telling everyone she was pregnant. And when the maid went into labor, the husband took her to the local hospital and signed her in as *his* wife, so the birth certificate would read that the child born to the maid was the *legitimate* child of the couple. Of course, it was an absurd idea, and completely illegal but, by some miracle, the ruse worked. No one suspected. The husband had told friends the delivery was difficult, and his wife could have no visitors until she returned home. While the maid was in the hospital masquerading as the wife, the real wife was hiding out in the maid's apartment across town."

"You're telling me you've found out who Maureen's baby is," Devlin said. "Why are you so down about it?

Is she the queen of England, or something? Would governments fall if the truth about the baby's birth were known?"

Laura shook her head, sighing listlessly. "No governments or thrones would fall. The child's not even rich—not yet, anyway."

"So, where is this lucky son of a bitch? In Ireland?"

"Yes..." she admitted, but her stomach clenched. She tried to hold on to her fragile control as she fumbled with the strings that tied the packet. Once the yellowed envelope was opened, she shuffled through it until she found what she was searching for. It was a bent and faded photograph, but clear enough to see the young, smiling woman clearly.

Handing it to Devlin, she murmured, "This is Maureen at nineteen. Lovely, isn't she?"

Devlin took the photograph from Laura's shaking fingers, frowning at her odd tremulousness. After scanning her face, he studied the picture.

"What do you think?" she managed, after a prolonged quiet that clawed at nerves that were already raw.

He stared at the photograph for a few seconds longer. When his eyes lifted, they burned coldly. "What the hell is this?" he demanded. "Some kind of joke?" Tossing the photograph down, he vaulted to his feet, confronting her. "What are you trying to tell me, Laura?"

She rescued the worn photo from being devoured by flames, her heart going out to him. "Did you see the necklace she had on?" she prodded. "Devlin, Maureen's mother, Vevila, told me there were only two of them ever made—by Maureen's father, a silversmith. He gave one to each of his daughters. Myrtle still wears hers." She took his arm to coax him to face her, for he had turned away. "Maureen had the other when she left home to work at Dingle Bay. Devlin . . . it's exactly like the Laughing Leprechaun you've worn since you were—"

"*No,*" he objected in a strangled voice. "It's too incredible, too much of a coincidence. I can't be the orphan. My parents wouldn't have lied to me all those years."

"They did an illegal thing. What could they do?" she defended softly. "You look like Maureen, Devlin. Your eyes—"

"To hell with my eyes." Grim-faced, he veered toward her, his jaw clenched. "I'm Devlin Rafferty, not some horny bastard's—" his lips twisted in a hateful sneer as he finished "—bastard. . . ."

"I have letters," she insisted, holding up three thin envelopes. "From your mother, Devlin. I mean—Mrs. Rafferty."

"She was my mother, dammit!" he shouted, then clamped his lips shut, as though trying to impose rigid control over his emotions.

Laura lifted the letters toward him. "I read them. It seems Maureen only asked one thing of the Raffertys, and that was that they visit Dingle Bay Country House at least every five years, and to let her know in advance, so she could take a room there at the same time. Just to see you. That was all she wanted, Devlin. To see her baby from time to time. I guess those were the secret trips she took the few times she left the foundling home—to get a glimpse of her little boy growing up. Do you remember her at all?"

His utter rejection of the idea was evident in the rage that tightened his jaw. "I don't believe any of this.

Where did this Vevila person come up with those letters after all these years, anyway?"

"I guess, when Maureen was ill at the end, she mailed home a silver jewel box her father had made for her as a child—one of her few precious possessions. Her mother, grief-stricken over Maureen's death, didn't look carefully at the box for years. But Vevila told me, about ten years ago, she found the letters in a secret compartment. Being a loving mother, she left them there in secret and never tried to contact the Raffertys. Since Maureen had repented her sin so completely, she felt there was no need to soil her reputation so long after her death." Laura took Devlin's hand, but he drew it away. She whispered, "I like Vevila, Devlin. You will, too. She'd be your grandmother, and she said she would be blessed if she could meet Maureen's child before she dies. She has two granddaughters that are Myrtle's children. But you are her only grandson."

He turned to glower at her, and with bridled anger in his voice, he declared, "Both of my grandmothers are dead."

"No, Devlin," she persisted. "You have a living grandmother. Look."

He glared at her with condemnation. "Nothing you say can make me believe . . ."

He trailed off, for Laura had held up another photograph. It was a picture of a little boy, about five years of age, and kneeling beside him was a smiling woman. She was fastening something about the child's neck.

"Mother . . ." he rasped, passing Laura a sidelong glance of disbelief. "Where did you get that?"

"It was in one of the letters. Mrs. Rafferty mailed it to Maureen after they gave you her Laughing Leprechaun on your fifth birthday. You told me about that, yourself. Remember?" she reminded him solemnly.

His shock was visible and genuine, and she felt a shaft of torment at having to be the one to destroy the only part of his world that he'd thought to be untainted. Even though Laura had told him more than once that no family was perfect, she felt no pleasure in proving it about his own family.

The parents he'd idolized hadn't even been his parents. What was worse, they'd done an illegal thing to gain a child and then lied to him all their lives. Devlin would have to deal with what he'd learned the best way he could. Just how, Laura wondered sadly, did one deal with learning that his "ideal" family was founded on illicit sex and long-buried lies?

He swore, dragging a hand through his hair. "Damn them! Damn them all!"

"But the money," she tried. "Devlin, you're a wealthy—"

With a bitter oath, he tore the silver chain from his neck, and Laura saw an angry red gash blossom across his throat where the broken chain had cut into his skin. He hurled the charm against the stones of the hearth. "Have a good laugh, you infernal pooka!" he ground out, his voice breaking with emotion. "You may have handed over your crock of gold, but you stole my history, my family, everything I—"

Breaking off with another curse, he dashed toward the door. "I have to think this out—alone," he muttered harshly.

The slamming of the door brought down a shower of plaster, making Laura cringe. When she realized that Devlin was running out into a cold, rainy night, she snatched up his sweatshirt and flung herself after him.

A steady rain slapped her face when she swung out the door onto the sidewalk, and her sweater was immediately soaked.

Catching him at the curb, she grabbed hold of his hand. "Devlin, I know you need to be by yourself, but . . ." She didn't know what to say to help, so with a helpless shake of her head, she handed him the sweatshirt, mumbling, "Don't catch cold."

"Don't catch—?" His laughter held both surprise and bitterness. "Why is it, that in the darkest moments we fall back on platitudes?" He snorted. "Don't catch a damn cold? Hell, Laura, my life has turned to garbage and you're telling me—" He grabbed the shirt and shrugged it on over his head. "There. Happy?"

As he tramped toward his car, she once again raced after him, taking hold of his shirtsleeve. "Devlin—I—" she stuttered. "I know this is a terrible time, but I have to tell you something else. . . ."

He turned on her, his features hostile, stark pain glimmering in his eyes. "More? What the hell now, an IRS audit?" he barked sarcastically.

Swiping her wet hair from her face, she shook her head. "It's about me. I—I should have told you before, Devlin, but things—I don't know. Things happened so quickly." He was watching her narrowly, his face bleak and hard, and her heart filled with cold, despairing guilt. "I—I have a daughter, Devlin." As his tortured eyes widened with disbelief, she flinched, her heart pounding with fear.

"You have a what?" he demanded, his face drawn with incredulity. "Why the hell didn't you tell me?"

Her teeth chattering from the damp cold, she reached into her slacks pocket for the picture she'd had ready. Pulling it out, she handed it to him, admitting raggedly, "Her name's S-Sally. She's—she's retarded. My only excuse for not telling you sooner is— Well, I figure my private life's none of anybody's business—"

"None of anybody's business?" he cut in, with shocked indignation. "My, you're a cool one. I tell you I want to marry you, and you say your retarded daughter is none of my damn business?" he charged roughly. "*Bull*, Laura." He slapped the photo back into her hand. "What the hell else haven't you told me that you're so ashamed of? Does your family have a congressman in the closet, maybe?"

"I—I'm not—ashamed, I . . ." She couldn't form any reasonable reply. His expression was gruesome, like that of someone who'd been kicked in the face. "I'm sorry, Devlin..." she cried, misery ripping through her. The tears she'd been holding in for so long, finally spilled unheeded from her eyes.

"Yeah, right," he scoffed. "You're sorry you lied. My folks were probably sorry *they* lied. I'll bet even Kevin-the-scumbag was sorry he had to lie so I'd save his worthless butt so he could go out and . . ."

His harsh laughter was full of anguish and rage. "Where in the hell did I get the arrogance to think I could read people?" he jeered in disgust. "I've got to be the damnedest, most gullible ass who ever walked the face of the earth!"

She saw his shudder of self-revulsion as he drew in a breath, but before she could react, he'd climbed into his rental car and was speeding away into the murky night.

Unable to hold it inside any longer, she wept aloud, hugging herself against the cold rain. "Goodbye, Devlin," she cried brokenly. "Goodbye, *acushla*...." The utter despair of her loss held her immobile for a long time. After a while, her benumbed glance fell on the rain-soaked photo in her hand. *Well,* she thought, as she stumbled listlessly toward the hotel door, *at least this time, you, little Sally, have been spared the heart-ache.*

When she reached the door, a savage grief flooded through her and she fell against the slippery jamb, reflexively covering her mouth with her hands to stanch sobs of desolation and regret. Yes, Sally had been spared, but somehow Laura knew *she* would never be free of heartache—ever again.

LAURA DIDN'T SEE DEVLIN again, after that night. She picked up the pieces of her heart as best she could, and went about her job verifying Devlin's right to the two million dollars, then she returned to Florida.

It took several weeks to settle the estate. Her boss had received a letter from the vice president of the trust department of a Chicago bank, with documentation that they were to handle the "Devlin Rafferty transfer of funds."

So, Laura hadn't even had a chance to speak to him. Among the official documents she'd mailed to his representatives at the bank were faded photos and letters as well as the Laughing Leprechaun, which she'd retrieved that horrible night after he'd left.

With their business concluded, she tried to return to her normal life, but Devlin's memory lingered doggedly, both in her dreams and, more disconcertingly, in unexpected, unwanted daydreams that interrupted her workdays more times than she cared to admit.

She hated herself for being so hung up on a man who didn't have the sensitivity to love a child like Sally. But even if he could have, he was in no shape for commitments right now—with his world in chaos. She decided she had to force him out of her mind, so, for the first time in years, she'd accepted a date. Tonight she was going out with a movie-theater manager named Boyd Clark.

He'd been bugging her to go out with him for over a year. And, after having known such intimate closeness with Devlin— Well, she was so terribly lonely. It had only been weeks since Devlin had driven away into the rainy night, but the time had dragged by like years. Unhappily, she realized that even a night out with bland Boyd Clark was better than another empty eternity alone with her poignant memories of a man who was lost to her forever.

She dreaded the prospect of dating, but she was flesh-and-blood human and couldn't live the rest of her life in a social vacuum. She needed someone, a relationship, and she might as well start meeting men again— try to make a life for herself and Sally. There had to be a guy out there who could love them both—a guy she could love the way she loved—

She bit her lip, wishing she didn't keep harking back to something that was over. . . .

The doorbell rang, and with a halfhearted sigh, she looked at her watch. Ten minutes till seven. Naturally, he'd be early. Hurriedly she put a comb through her hair, sweeping the curly stuff to one side, away from her face, and giving it a haphazard pat. She recalled the last time she'd overdried her perm. It had been exactly this frizzy, and Devlin, with those sad yet amused eyes, had honestly seemed to like it that way. With a determined shake of her head, she pushed up from her chair. This was no time to dredge up futile, sentimental memories. Boyd was here.

Anyway, Boyd wouldn't mind about her hair. He owned a crazy collection of campy ties with scenes of old sitcoms, like *I Love Lucy* and *The Brady Bunch* on them. What would a little frizz mean to a guy like that? He'd probably love it. She only wished she could say the same thing about him.

Unable to keep the wistfulness from her voice, she called to Sally, "Honey, Mommy's friend is here, but the baby-sitter's not. We won't leave till she comes, but can you get into your pj's by yourself?"

"I—try," came Sally's high-pitched voice.

"Good girl," Laura encouraged, rushing along the short hall to the apartment entry.

Swinging the door wide, she said, "Boyd, you're earl—" She came to a bewildered halt, completely losing her train of thought. Instead of a slender redhead with a handlebar mustache and a crazy tie, stood— stood . . .

"Devlin?" she breathed, taking in his tall, elegantly proportioned physique and powerful shoulders. A familiar half smile, as intimate as a kiss, curved his lips, and those eyes—so brilliantly blue, direct and tender— seemed vaguely cautious, as though he wasn't quite sure he would be welcome.

"I gather you were expecting Boyd and Earl?" he asked with a inquiring lift of one brow.

She swallowed. "I—I— Only Boyd. I thought he was early," she explained inanely. There were so many things crowding her brain that she wanted to say, and discussing a meaningless date wasn't one of them.

"Maybe I should come back some other time," he suggested, but made no move to go.

"No!" she cried, then blanched, trying to get herself under control. She had no idea why he might be here.

Nothing had been resolved between them. Inhaling deeply, she said more calmly, "Well, you could come on in. Boyd won't be here for a few more minutes."

Devlin stepped into the apartment, closing the door. "So you have a date?" he inquired.

She nodded and shrugged, feeling self-conscious. "He's a pleasant-enough man."

"Is he?" Devlin queried, surveying her modest residence.

"Yes," she replied, without much conviction.

"Nice place," Devlin commented.

"Thanks . . ."

There was a minute of silence while they looked at each other. Laura became skittish under his scrutiny and finally blurted, "Well—I have a right to date, don't I!"

He thrust his hands into his slacks pockets, murmuring, "Sure."

She hesitated, blinking with confusion. "Devlin, why have you come?" she finally managed. "Boyd will be here any second. How do I explain you?"

Her question seemed to amuse him, for he pursed his lips as though masking a grin. "Why didn't you tell me you liked your men with wild ties?"

"Well," she shook her head in exasperation. "I don't particular—" With a start, she squinted up at him, dubious. "What makes you ask a question like that?"

His lips twitched. "I have a confession." There was no hint of repentance in his voice.

She grew watchful. "What have you done?"

He indicated the door. "I met Boyd in the hallway, and I—convinced him to leave."

She gaped. "You— What did you do to him?"

He lifted a shoulder, smiling wryly. "I flipped him for you."

"You—you didn't!" she gasped, appalled. "That's— that's barbaric. That's stone-age! You don't flip for a woman like you'd flip for a—a lunch tab!"

Scanning her with eyes that were both tender and teasing, he asked, "Don't you want to know who won the toss?"

His question caught her off guard and she blinked in confusion, then realized he was joking. With a smirk of disdain, she said, "That's very funny. I'd forgotten how hysterical you can be."

Openly amused now, he suggested, "You might still be able to catch your date with the wild tie if you run."

"Don't think I won't," she warned, lifting an obstinate chin. "You'd better have a good reason for such uncivil behavior."

"I guess I thought proposing to you in front of the guy might make him uncomfortable."

She'd opened her lips to protest whatever ridiculous reason he came up with, but his softly-spoken answer stunned her to silence.

One long stride brought him very close. He pulled her against him, whispering huskily against her ear, "*Acushla*. I've been a damned fool. It's taken me a while to work things out in my mind, but I've forgiven my folks for their lies. I spent some time alone, going through old photo albums, remembering—trying to put myself in their place. I can't fault them for being human. Wanting children. Dammit, they gave me a wonderful life." His voice was rough with emotion. "Now, I have to know if you can forgive me for being such an unfeeling jerk. About your daughter. I should have known it was something like that—some painful reason why you were leery of getting close to another man."

Feeling the sting of tears, she drew her lips between her teeth to keep them from trembling as he said, "I want to meet your little girl."

She pulled away, looking up at his face, indistinct through her tears. "But—but you were so disgusted in the foundling home by that retarded girl. Devlin, don't try to change your attitude for me. It—it won't work in the long run. You'll—you'll leave us—" Her voice broke.

"*Hell*," he rasped bitterly, dragging her even more closely into his possessive embrace. "I was disgusted by the way she'd been treated, Laura. Not by the little girl." Withdrawing slightly, he gazed down at her, his eyes stormy with pain. "You really thought it was because of the girl?"

She gulped hard, but couldn't form words. When she could only nod, he growled out his frustration, "All my stupid talk about the perfect family scared you off. Oh, Laura, if I'd known how I was hurting you, I'd have cut out my damn tongue!" Lowering his face to hers, he kissed her gently, and when she looked into his eyes, she sensed the unconditional honesty of his words.

"Oh—Devlin—"

Her frail cry was interrupted by a muffled pitter-patter sound, and they both turned toward it. Sally hop-skipped toward them. The footed Mickey Mouse pajamas she wore were skewed oddly. Probably because she'd managed to get both arms and one leg in properly, but had missed the other leg entirely, leaving the chubby appendage bare, and a limp streamer of footed fabric wagging against her hip like a misplaced tail.

"Mama?" she said, screwing up her face. "Can't do—wifout you."

Unable to help herself, Laura cast Devlin a worried look, and was astonished to see him grinning down at Sally. Catching her concerned perusal, he winked, saying softly under his breath, "Out of the mouths of babes . . ."

His completely accepting smile filled Laura with joy. Suddenly she felt a great weight lift from her shoulders. No longer was she alone. And amazingly, in that one, telling glance, Sally had been totally accepted. Unable to put her feeling into words, Laura gave him a quick peck on the cheek and bent to help her daughter.

HOURS LATER, LONG AFTER Sally had gone to sleep, Laura snuggled against Devlin, kissing his chest as she admitted softly, "Okay, Devlin. I believe . . ."

He turned on the pillow, grazing her forehead with warm lips. "What do you believe?"

"In your leprechauns, of course. Watching you with Sally tonight, I could believe in anything wonderful and mythical and crazy."

With a soft chuckle, he slid over her. The Laughing Leprechaun, repaired and hanging about his neck, tickled her breasts. "And there's that other miracle," he reminded, teasing her with his lips.

"What other miracle?" she asked, kissing back.

"That Sally's a heavy sleeper."

"That howling was *your* fault, you know," she said, giggling.

His answering chuckle was deep and sensual. "I think we're going to have to buy a big, isolated house," he suggested. "Do you think Florida might need a Prince of the Underdogs?"

She curled her arms about his broad chest. "I don't know about Florida. But *I* do."

"We'll start looking for a big old isolated house with plenty of grounds, maybe a fishing pond—for the kids."

"Kids?" she teased, with every intention of giving this man the family he wanted—that they both wanted.

He nibbled at her earlobe. "What do you think about kids?"

"Devlin!" Relishing the sexy feel of his lips and tongue, she sighed. "Let's talk exact numbers later...."

"After the honeymoon." His tongue trailed enticingly along her chin.

"What honeymoon?" she asked through a tremulous moan of pleasure.

"The extended one we're taking to Ireland." He nipped at her throat, sending ripples of delight through her. "If you agree, I'd like to give an endowment of one million dollars to the Galway Foundling Home, and—" He paused, then suddenly solemn, added, "And I have family to meet."

A tear escaped the outer corner of her eye, and she hugged him tighter. "I'm glad, Devlin. And I think the money would be a lovely gift."

"It's the least I can do," he said quietly. "They reunited me with my—my heritage."

She hugged him consolingly. "You're okay with it?"

"Yeah," he said, kissing her chin. "With you beside me, it'll all settle into place."

A tiny, foolish worry niggled at Laura's brain. She hoped it was tiny and foolish, but she had to ask. Haltingly, she cleared her throat. "What will we do with Sally—on this honeymoon?"

"She goes, of course. She's family." He shifted into a very delightful, familiar position above her, making her gasp. Fairly quivering with anticipation, she breathed, "I—I love you so...."

"I've always loved you." The touch of his lips sent a delicious sensation along her shoulder. "We could drop by the International Bachelors Festival," he whispered with a grin. She felt a crazy stab of jealousy, but she had no time to debate, as he added, "I thought you'd want to cheer for Ogan. Second runner-up takes my place."

Feeling suddenly quite wonderful, like a bold temptress, she slid her hands down over his hips, relishing the feel of strong, tightly drawn muscles as he began his gentle stroking. "Nobody could ever take your place," she murmured sensuously.

As he worked his erotic magic, his expression soft yet compelling, Laura knew that at last Devlin had found peace within his soul. And she sighed, not only with the sultry ecstasy he was inducing, but with the knowledge that their union would be blessed with a special breed of happiness. Their Laughing Leprechaun, who had brought them miraculously together, would guard their hearth evermore....

HARLEQUIN®
Temptation®
IS TEN!

Join the festivities as Harlequin celebrates
Temptation's tenth anniversary in 1994!

Look for tempting treats from your favorite
Temptation authors all year long. The celebration
begins with Passion's Quest—four exciting sensual
stories featuring the most elemental passions....

The temptation continues with Lost Loves, a sizzling
miniseries about love lost...love found. And watch for
the 500th Temptation in July by bestselling author
Rita Clay Estrada, a seductive story in the vein
of the much-loved tale, THE IVORY KEY.

In May, look for details of an irresistible offer:
three classic Temptation novels by Rita Clay Estrada,
Glenda Sanders and Gina Wilkins in a collector's
hardcover edition—free with proof of purchase!

After ten tempting years, *nobody* can resist

Temptation®

HTIOAN

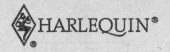

Harlequin proudly presents four stories about *convenient* but not *conventional* reasons for marriage:

- ◆ To save your godchildren from a "wicked stepmother"

- ◆ To help out your eccentric aunt—and her sexy business partner

- ◆ To bring an old man happiness by making him a grandfather

- ◆ To escape from a ghostly existence and become a real woman

Marriage By Design—four brand-new stories by four of Harlequin's most popular authors:

CATHY GILLEN THACKER
JASMINE CRESSWELL
GLENDA SANDERS
MARGARET CHITTENDEN

Don't miss this exciting collection of stories about marriages of convenience. Available in April, wherever Harlequin books are sold.

MBD94

Earth, Wind, Fire, Water
The four elements—but nothing is
more elemental than passion

Join us for Passion's Quest, four sizzling action-packed romances
in the tradition of *Romancing the Stone* and *The African Queen*.
Starting in January 1994, one Temptation each month is a sexy,
romantic adventure focusing on the quest for passion....

On sale in April

Escape the gray gloom of April showers with *Undercurrent* by
Lisa Harris. Susannah Finley had always played it safe—too safe.
So when FBI agent Gus Raphael called in a favor, she didn't
hesitate. He needed her help on a sting operation. It was the
chance to have the adventure of a lifetime. And who knew *what*
close contact with Gus would lead to?

If you missed any Harlequin Temptation Passion's Quest titles, here's your
chance to order them:

#473	BODY HEAT by Elise Title	$2.99	☐
#477	WILD LIKE THE WIND by Janice Kaiser	$2.99	☐
#481	AFTERSHOCK by Lynn Michaels	$2.99	☐

TOTAL AMOUNT	$ _____
POSTAGE & HANDLING	$ _____
($1.00 for one book, 50¢ for each additional)	
APPLICABLE TAXES*	$ _____
TOTAL PAYABLE	$ _____
(check or money order—please do not send cash)	

To order, complete this form and send it, along with a check or money order for the total
above, payable to Harlequin Books, to: **In the U.S.:** 3010 Walden Avenue,
P.O. Box 9047, Buffalo, NY 14269-9047; **In Canada:** P.O. Box 613, Fort Erie, Ontario,
L2A 5X3.

Name: _____
Address: _____ City: _____
State/Prov.: _____ Zip/Postal Code: _____

*New York residents remit applicable sales taxes.
Canadian residents remit applicable GST and provincial taxes.   HTPQ3

Temptation®

HARLEQUIN®

Don't miss these Harlequin favorites by some of our most distinguished authors!
And now, you can receive a discount by ordering two or more titles!

HT#25409	THE NIGHT IN SHINING ARMOR by JoAnn Ross	$2.99	☐
HT#25471	LOVESTORM by JoAnn Ross	$2.99	☐
HP#11463	THE WEDDING by Emma Darcy	$2.89	☐
HP#11592	THE LAST GRAND PASSION by Emma Darcy	$2.99	☐
HR#03188	DOUBLY DELICIOUS by Emma Goldrick	$2.89	☐
HR#03248	SAFE IN MY HEART by Leigh Michaels	$2.89	☐
HS#70464	CHILDREN OF THE HEART by Sally Garrett	$3.25	☐
HS#70524	STRING OF MIRACLES by Sally Garrett	$3.39	☐
HS#70500	THE SILENCE OF MIDNIGHT by Karen Young	$3.39	☐
HI#22178	SCHOOL FOR SPIES by Vickie York	$2.79	☐
HI#22212	DANGEROUS VINTAGE by Laura Pender	$2.89	☐
HI#22219	TORCH JOB by Patricia Rosemoor	$2.89	☐
HAR#16459	MACKENZIE'S BABY by Anne McAllister	$3.39	☐
HAR#16466	A COWBOY FOR CHRISTMAS by Anne McAllister	$3.39	☐
HAR#16462	THE PIRATE AND HIS LADY by Margaret St. George	$3.39	☐
HAR#16477	THE LAST REAL MAN by Rebecca Flanders	$3.39	☐
HH#28704	A CORNER OF HEAVEN by Theresa Michaels	$3.99	☐
HH#28707	LIGHT ON THE MOUNTAIN by Maura Seger	$3.99	☐

Harlequin Promotional Titles

#83247	YESTERDAY COMES TOMORROW by Rebecca Flanders	$4.99	☐
#83257	MY VALENTINE 1993	$4.99	☐
	(short-story collection featuring Anne Stuart, Judith Arnold, Anne McAllister, Linda Randall Wisdom)		

(limited quantities available on certain titles)

	AMOUNT	$
DEDUCT:	10% DISCOUNT FOR 2+ BOOKS	$
ADD:	POSTAGE & HANDLING	$
	($1.00 for one book, 50¢ for each additional)	
	APPLICABLE TAXES*	$ _____
	TOTAL PAYABLE	$ _____
	(check or money order—please do not send cash)	

To order, complete this form and send it, along with a check or money order for the total above, payable to Harlequin Books, to: **In the U.S.:** 3010 Walden Avenue, P.O. Box 9047, Buffalo, NY 14269-9047; **In Canada:** P.O. Box 613, Fort Erie, Ontario, L2A 5X3.

Name: _____

Address: _____ City: _____

State/Prov.: _____ Zip/Postal Code: _____

*New York residents remit applicable sales taxes.
 Canadian residents remit applicable GST and provincial taxes.

HBACK-JM